# For the Love of
# Thomas Amore

## A novella by Charles H. Roberts III

NFB
Buffalo, New York

Front cover designed © by MacLaine Russell.  For more information
visit http://www.mcln.net/

Back cover photo © by Jeffrey T. Barnes.  For more information visit
http://www.jeffreytbarnesphotography.com/

NFB
<<<>>>
No Frills Buffalo/Amelia Press
119 Dorchester Road
Buffalo, New York 14213

For more information visit

nfbpublishing.com

A big thank-you goes out to my wonderful wife, April, who never batted an eye at my late nights in the home office while writing this book (mostly because her eyes were shut). But in all seriousness, without her encouragement and willingness to listen to me talk through multiple changes to the plot, the pages that follow would likely still be an unfinished manuscript.

And certainly, I would be remiss if I didn't acknowledge my friends and family – all of whom have been more than willing to lend an ear through the years…whether it had anything to do with this book or otherwise.

# For the Love of Thomas Amore

# ONE:
## WAKE-UP CALL

It was January of 2014, and Thomas Amore woke up in a panic.

He reached to the left and doubled back to the right, searching for his wooden box – a small, handheld gathering point for his precious few belongings.

"Where is it?" he screamed, saliva stringing along his weathered gray beard – and a rare bit of profanity spewing from his mouth. "Where the hell is it?"

He panned the drifting eyes and crooked smiles that filled the room. Hunched over by the window and illuminated by the sun's sparkle off the morning snowfall, he noticed a man sifting through the box, which mostly contained a collection of letters and his poetry.

"Hey! Get your paws off that!" Amore yelled, anger beaming from his eyes.

He lived only where he could find shelter, with life as a minute-by-minute struggle.

Amore charged toward the man, hurdling the scattering of mattresses along the way. A little less than halfway, a woman awoke, jumping up as he leapt over her. The arch of her back interrupted his frantic pace, sending him to a face-first fall.

Slightly dazed, his ears ringing, he stood up and reached to his eyebrow.

With blood streaming down his cheek, he continued to his target, screaming even more furiously than before. The man, startled by Amore's appearance, stood still and removed his hands from the box.

"Give me that!" Amore screamed, blood dripping from his brow and with a steady stream of saliva launching from his mouth. "Give me that!"

Trembling, Amore rummaged through the box, ensuring the contents hadn't been compromised.

"Okay," he said, rocking slightly on his knees. "It's all here... it's all here."

He pressed the sleeve of his coat – a relic of his army service – against his eye to halt the bleeding. But after such a chaotic scene, he certainly wasn't about to stick around for a day at the homeless shelter; it was onto the streets to battle Mother Nature and plead for his next meal.

Bursting out of the shelter's side door, he was met immediately by the reality of the northern winter. The wind screamed into the building, blowing the light snow from the ground onto the floor inside.

"Hey! Shut that door!" one man yelled, exposing a horribly corroded smile. "It's freezing, for god's sake!"

Amore stumbled out into the cold, his coat half-zipped. With the box under his arm, he drifted toward the business district in hopes of panhandling enough money to buy a cup of coffee and a bagel.

His outburst notwithstanding, Amore wasn't considered to be much of an aggressive man. In fact, his approach to panhandling – or lack thereof – seldom yielded enough money to score a meal at one of the area's coffee shops.

The bench from which he often attempted to secure funding was right in the thick of the city's heaviest foot traffic. But given his vagrant appearance – a straggly beard and clothes that weren't exactly cleaned the day prior – his efforts more often than not went overlooked.

"Spare some change for a Vietnam veteran?" he'd ask, quietly.

He never got too deep into telling or selling his story, so to speak. If one out of every 10 or 15 people he asked dropped his or her change, Amore was content. He'd never been one for haggling.

On that particular day, however, it was as though the plug had been pulled. He sat there in silence while the aggressively falling snow pelted his recently battered face. He could feel his pulse reverberating through the walls of his skull. Through the silence he sat, though the voices of memories from afar seemed ever so present.

He needed change, he thought – and not just the kind that would jingle in the bottom of a cup.

*Personal & Confidential*

*Date: Unknown*

*It seems like just yesterday I was running free, a 17-year-old who was in total control of my mental and physical well-being.*

*My future seemed so bright. People believed in me, and equally as important – I believed in myself.*

*Things were going to be just fine. I'd have love, financial success and maybe – just maybe – a bit of fame.*

*--From the journal of Thomas Amore*

# Two:
# Rising Star

For the first 17 years of his life, Thomas "Tom" Amore faced adversity head-on.

He was just 4 years old when his father passed away, the result of an on-the-job accident at the steel mill. And although his mother inexplicably maintained employment through the years, she spent the bulk of her non-working hours in an alcohol-induced haze.

As a boy, Amore was often left to fend for himself. On the surface, he seemed to be a diamond in the rough. But that began unraveling in the summer of 1965.

Amore was participating in two-a-day workouts for the School 16 Cats, a high school football team in Buffalo, N.Y.

He was an incredible athlete. Although he was the team's starting tailback, he had the ability to line up at just about any position on the field.

He was widely considered the team's leader, and it was a foregone conclusion that Division I college football was in his very near future.

"Gentlemen, you are looking at a Division I player right here," Bill McBride, the Cats' head coach, said after the first practice that summer.

McBride was a fierce man. He stood an even six feet and had a cutting jaw, a bald head, and ropes for veins that protruded from his muscular arms. The pot of black coffee he drank each morning stained his teeth horribly, only further fueling an already intense demeanor.

He gave the impression that he was not to be liked, but he was to be respected. He also gave the impression that he probably didn't like you.

But he liked Amore.

He liked that Amore showed up to practice an hour early to stretch, run a few laps around the track, and already had sweat visible not only before the other players arrived, but, often, the coaching staff.

McBride was as close to a father figure as Amore ever had.

He first took interest in Amore when he saw him as a seventh grader tossing the ball around in the park next to the Cats' practice field. McBride stayed in close contact with him from that day forward, before finally getting him on the football team once he was in high school.

Amore became the first freshman to join the varsity team in the school's history.

The players didn't dare question McBride's loyalty to Amore despite his bullish approach to the rest of the group. There always seemed to be an unspoken respect for his fatherless home and the unrivaled enthusiasm that he brought to the game.

The first day of practice was no walk in the park. The sun was uninterrupted amid the otherwise all-blue sky while temperatures roared in at a blistering 91 degrees.

"Tom, we're gonna die out here, man," said quarterback Walter Higgins. "It's too hot."

"Nah, we're gonna be just fine, Walt," Amore said calmly. "Stay hydrated and stay focused."

McBride ran the team to the point of exhaustion. At one point during "suicides" – an incremental run – 11 players were keeled over and vomiting in near unison.

"Let's go, ladies!" McBride yelled, his cheeks fire-engine red.

Amore finished ahead of the pack; he stood with his hands on top of his helmet and waited for the rest of the team.

As practice ended that day, all 67 players trying to make the squad knelt down on one knee, helmets by their side. McBride, still standing, made it clear that Amore was their leader – a man among boys.

"Men, as we sit here, most of you look like you want to quit," McBride said. "You're desperate for water and probably a handful of pain meds. Well, I want you to look into your souls. Ask yourself: 'Am I a leader or a follower? Am I the kind of person who will never quit on my fellow man?' If you are indeed a follower, there is one person I want you following; and that is Thomas Amore."

A few of the boys chuckled.

"Shut up, guys! Coach is talking. Show some respect," Amore interrupted.

"That's the kind of thing I'm talking about," McBride said. "And going back to what I was saying, if you are the kind of person who quits on his fellow man, then walk your sorry butt off this field at once!"

The group went silent. A few heads turned, panning to see if anyone was going to walk off. After a minute filled with only the sound of football equipment creaking, McBride blew the final whistle.

"Okay, gentlemen," he said. "I will see you here tomorrow. I want everyone to put a little extra salt on their food tonight to avoid cramping. And for the love of God: stay out of trouble."

As they walked off the field, Higgins ran to catch up with Amore.

"Hey, Amore, hold up," he said, carrying his helmet in his left hand and waving him down with his right.

He halted his fast-walk pace to the locker room and stopped to un-buckle his chinstrap.

"How do you do it, man?" Higgins asked.

"Do what, Walt?" Amore asked.

"You know: keep up the cool and collected attitude? I mean, it's like a million degrees out here today and Coach is being a total jerk," Higgins said.

"Walt, you just gotta understand that Coach only wants to win," Amore said. "He doesn't care that it's too hot – that's only an excuse to him. Think about it. Our job is only to come out here and work hard for three hours. It doesn't matter if it's hot, cold, or somewhere in between. We just need to focus on what it takes to be better football players. So who really cares if Coach is riding you or yelling at you? We're out here to play a game - one that we love, right?"

"Yeah. You are right, Tom. I just, well, you know – sometimes it's hard to keep things in perspective," Higgins said.

"So do I have your commitment, then, Walt? If you focus, I know we can make this team a state championship contender. I can't do it alone," Amore said.

"Definitely. I'm with you, Tom," Walt said with conviction.

The two slapped an aggressive high-five-turned-half-hug and made their way to the locker room. But as they trotted toward the school, McBride yelled over to Amore.

"Hey, four," he shouted, referring to Amore's jersey number. "Come here for a second."

Amore broke off from Higgins and made his way over to McBride, who was waiting with his clipboard in hand.

"What's up, Coach?" he asked.

"I've got some exciting news, kid," McBride said. "Tomorrow morning is a day you and I have been waiting for from the first day I met you."

"What is it, sir?" Amore asked, tilting his helmet up to wipe the sweat from his brow.

"Recruiters from Syracuse and Penn State are coming down to meet with you and watch you practice tomorrow. You are on your way, young man," McBride said.

"Oh, boy, Coach! That's incredible!" Amore said.

They hugged as though they were father and son, and McBride gave him some final instructions.

"Go straight home," he said. "Here are a few pamphlets from both schools. At least read these, if nothing else. They have some of the basic information. It wouldn't hurt to be at least somewhat educated as to their history."

"Yes, sir," Amore said. "See you tomorrow, Coach!"

As he made his way through the set of double doors behind the gym which led to the locker room, a few of his teammates were waiting.

"Hey, Amore, my man," said offensive lineman Michael DiBenditti.

"Is it true?"

"Is what true?" Amore asked, a smirk drawn across his face.

"Come on, man. We heard that 15 D-I schools are coming to meet with you tomorrow," DiBenditti said.

"Nah, fellas," Amore said.

"Come on, Amore," said wide receiver Steve Russell. "Just tell us."

"Okay already," he said. "Syracuse and Penn State are coming."

"No way!" DiBenditti excitedly interrupted.

"Keep it quiet, man. I don't want Coach to know you guys know," Amore said. "You know how he is. He doesn't like gossip and all that."

"Listen, there's a party over at Lila Stevenson's tonight," Russell said. "You should come celebrate. There's gonna be tons of chicks and, most importantly, whiskey."

"You know I don't drink," Amore said. "Plus, I have to read and get ready for tomorrow."

"Man... what's to get ready?" Russell asked with a puzzled look on his face. "You are Tom Amore, the most pure athlete this area has ever seen. You don't need to get ready – you already are."

"Sorry, Russell, maybe next time," Amore said as he continued walking toward the locker room.

"Fine, but you'll regret it when I'm getting some later and you're home listening to the radio," Russell yelled down the hall.

Amore took his time showering after practice. He had quite a bit on his mind. Despite the leadership skills he conveyed, he was a nervous wreck on the inside. He was scared that his mother – a sunken-faced drunk – might act irrationally when he broke the news that a couple of big schools were after him.

He feared that the first thing out of her mouth might be about the cost of either school if a full scholarship wasn't offered. Being a single mother, she didn't have much in the way of money.

And as her drinking got heavier, so did her level of self-pity.

Amore finally left the school and biked home that evening at around 6:30 – a solid 30 minutes after everyone else had cleared out.

He avoided the main streets to elude traffic and, more importantly, noise. He wanted 100 percent silence on the way home to clear his mind and think of how he was going to share what everyone considered good news to his mother, who he fully expected to be in a state of alcohol-induced inebriation.

As he peddled, the wheels were spinning equally as fast in his head. The sound of the summer breeze whistled in his ears.

Amore's heart raced as he rounded the corner and turned onto his street.

Much to his surprise, however, his mother's car was not in the driveway.

He pulled up and gradually slid to a stop as the brakes squealed.

He set the bike down and soon discovered surprise number two: an unlocked, wide open door.

"Mom?" he asked. "Hello... anybody home? Mom?"

Nothing.

Like most kids after school, Amore's next move was to peruse the contents of the refrigerator. He pulled out a bowl of leftover pasta and set it on the counter.

Then it dawned on him: Perhaps she had left a note. He looked in the usual spots – the front of the refrigerator, the kitchen table, the counter, and by the telephone.

Once again – nothing.

The pasta stood no chance. He ended up eating every last bit, leaving only remnants of the seasoning at the bottom of the bowl.

He sat at the table and pulled out pamphlets for each university.

"Syracuse University," he said quietly to himself.

"Ladies and gentlemen, from Buffalo, New York, number four, Tom Amoooooooooore!" He proclaimed, pretending to be a public address announcer.

Amore smiled and nodded his head in contentment.

Then he pulled out the Penn State pamphlet.

"Okay, Penn State, let's see what you're about," he said, once again to himself.

"The Penn State Nittany Lions are proud to have appeared in six Bowl games, including four straight from 1959-1962, winning three of them. The Nittany Lions' roar will soon be heard around the nation. Become a part of something special; be a part of the next championship team," he read aloud from the pamphlet.

He set the pamphlet back on the table and looked toward the door – still no sign of his mother. He looked back at the two pamphlets, sitting side by side. A bit anxious, he began tapping his fingers on the table.

Amore sat in complete silence for another minute or two, but he needed a distraction of some sort. The nearby radio might do just the trick, he thought.

He caught the tail end of "The Adventures of Ozzie and Harriet," a re-run from before its switch to television. There was no television in the two-person Amore residence. The program brought out a bit of laughter, but he soon returned to silence as a talk-radio program came on next.

The silence, as they say, was deafening. Amore's mind was accelerating but headed in no particular direction. *Syracuse or Penn State? What will Mom think of the schools? Is she even okay? What are the guys from the team doing? Are there girls there? Where on earth is my mother?* he thought.

Amore's head was seemingly ready to burst when suddenly the phone rang.

"H-hello," he stammered, his mind still racing.

*May 3, 1969*

*Tom-*

*Before you head off to war, I wanted to leave you with something to look back upon. Maybe these words will help you during a tough time; maybe you'll throw this letter in the trash. Only you know, I suppose.*

*Anyhow...*

*Don't ever forget where you came from. It was your ability to block out the nonsense that made you one of the toughest people that I've ever met. But you also shouldn't forget about the mistake; let it be a lesson that every decision you make alters part of your future.*

*With that being said, I also don't want you to ever dwell on the past. What's done is done, and the best is yet to come – if you're willing to continuously put one foot in front of the other and keep moving forward, even when it feels like the weight of the world is holding you back.*

*I know life didn't always deal you the best cards, but somehow – even after the mistake – it still seemed like you had an ace in your pocket. Never let go of that ace.*

*I'm a letter away while you're gone, and my door is always open when you return. Make me proud, boy.*

*Best,*
*Bill McBride*

## THREE:
## THE CALL THAT CHANGED IT ALL

It was a day that he'd never forget.

He'd never forget that darn phone ringing, as he'd say often, later in life.

Why in the world did the phone have to ring? And better yet, why did he answer it?

"Amore, my man; it's Russell," said the guy on the other end.

"Uh, hey... what's up, man?" Amore responded.

"This party is. All the cheerleaders are here and want to hear about your big day tomorrow," Russell said, with what sounded like chaos in the background.

"Is there drinking going on?" Amore asked.

"Yeah, but who cares, man – just get over here!" Russell said.

Amore sat there in a moment of silence, weighing his options.

"Amore? You there?" Russell asked.

And that was the first step toward the end of his life.

"Yeah, buddy. I'll try to make it. What's the address?" Amore asked.

"617 Rochester Street... get over here!" Russell said.

"Okay. I'm just kind of waiting on my mom to get home," Amore said. "I'll give it a few minutes. If she's not home soon, I'll probably head over."

Amore ran to the back of the house where his bedroom was, pretending to out-maneuver would-be football defenders the whole way. He'd run for a state record, 1,432 yards, as a junior; certainly no would-be air defender was going to take him down.

"He could... go... all... the... way," Amore said to himself. "Touchdown, Amore!"

When he got to his bedroom, he glanced into the closet, still debating whether or not to go to the party at Lila Stevenson's house. He grabbed a polo shirt and khakis and tossed them onto his bed before taking a seat at his desk.

Sitting at his desk, Amore looked in the mirror. He ran his hand across his chin, which had a bit of rash from the chinstrap of his football helmet.

"Do I go to this party or don't I?" he said, again to himself. "What to do, what to do..."

About 10 seconds later, he heard the front door open. He retraced his steps, again pretending to run like a football player, to the front of the house.

"Hey, Mom! I've been waiting to share some great news! Where have you been?" he asked.

"Don't you go and worry 'bout what I'm-a-doin'," she said, reeking of Scotch and cigarette smoke.

"Mom, I just wanted to tell you," Amore said, before being interrupted.

"What is it, kid? You gonna be a big football star like your father wanted to be?" she asked in a drunken, sarcastic manner.

And just like that, he made a firm decision to attend the party. If he was to be in the presence of a drunk, it might as well be someone who appreciated him, he thought.

"You know what? I'm going to hang with some friends. I guess I'll just catch up with you some other time, Mom," Amore said.

"Whatever... I gotta get me a..." she said, trailing off and making little sense.

With that, Amore walked out the front door. He had seen, smelled, and heard enough.

"Darn it," he mumbled to himself as he got on his bike. "What a stinking drunk."

He pedaled ferociously, a wide range of emotions spinning through his head nearly as quickly as the tires spun underneath him.

The second he got off his bike, however, and saw a group of his teammates, cheerleaders, and various other students waiting for his arrival outside of Stevenson's house, his mindset changed.

His drunken mother was a distant memory. His big day to come was further up the road. In living for the moment – at least for this instance – Amore felt acceptance. He felt appreciated. He felt loved by someone other than his football coach.

"Amoreeeeeeeeee," Stevenson playfully pronounced his name, as Amore walked up to the house.

"Hey, guys," Amore said, somewhat humbled but smiling.

"Give my man a drink," Russell said.

"Nah. You know I don't drink, pal," Amore said.

"Okay, okay," Russell said, backing down. "Well, let's go out back and hit the pool."

Whether he liked it or not, Amore was the center of attention. As he prepared to take his shirt off to jump in the pool, a group of girls whispered and giggled together, pointing in his direction.

"What, what is it?" Amore asked.

"Well, it's just that we want to see you with your shirt off," one admitted.

"What's the big deal?" Amore asked, blushing a bit.

"Let's see what you're made of, Mr. Football Man," another girl called out.

He laughed again, rather humbled, took his shirt off, and hopped in the pool. Instantly there was a school of girls swimming his way. Although he was a team leader on the football field, this was not the type of attention Amore was used to.

"Now, now, ladies," he said, joking.

"Oh, you're so cute," quipped a girl whom he had never met.

You'd never know it by looking at the present-day Thomas Amore, but his frame was chiseled back then. He spent a great deal of time lifting weights and running to prepare for football season.

The smile grew on his face with the attention his shirtless body was receiving.

"Hey, ladies – shots of whiskey," Russell said, lining up a row of six whiskey-filled shot glasses.

The sun was beginning to fade into the late summer sky. Amore glanced at the whiskey and found himself in a rare position as he began to second-guess himself.

*Maybe this will take my mind of things at home*, he thought. *No... that's stupid; I should resist. But then again, I wonder what all the fuss is about?*

"Thomas, are you in?" Stevenson asked.

Amore drifted backward in the water, slowly crashing his back into the far wall of the pool, then holding himself up with his elbows on the rail.

"Nah. I'm just going to relax," he said.

"Come on, Amore, we gotta celebrate!" Russell demanded.

"Yeah, come on, Thomas – get over here," Stevenson insisted.

Amore thrust himself off the back wall and swam over in breast-stroke form. As he crawled up onto the deck, Stevenson immediately got his attention.

"There's my little football hunk," she said, grabbing hold of Amore's arm.

He sat there thinking of ways to avoid taking the shot of whiskey.

Perhaps he could toss it over his shoulder, he thought.

Suddenly, Stevenson handed him the glass. The pressure was on.

"Cheers," she proclaimed.

There was no turning back at this point. There was no faking it, either.

Just hours earlier, Amore had lamented the sight and sounds of his intoxicated mother – and yet there he was, following in her footsteps.

*Okay... maybe just one*, he thought. *What harm can that do?*

They clanked glasses together in celebration and down the shots went.

The group let out a collective cringe and nearly all of them simultaneously let out a gag-reflux sound.

"Aw... it burns," Amore said in disgust.

*Never again*, he thought. Just one and done.

"Let's do another," Stevenson said. "That was nothing."

*The heck with it*, he thought.

Soon after, they clanked glasses again. And then again. Before long, the entire group was drunk – hammered.

As the rookie drinker of the group, Amore was far and away the most intoxicated, however.

"Come on, Thomas. Let's get you inside for a bit," Stevenson said, grabbing hold of his arm as he swayed in mid-conversation.

"B-b-but I was jus' tellin' these guys about my mother an' how I got this meeting in the morn'... morn'... morning," Amore said, sounding like a weathered drunk at a corner bar.

"Come on, sweetie. Let's get you inside," Stevenson responded.

The two walked arm-in-arm into the house and made their way to the kitchen.

"We need to get some food in you," Stevenson said. "I heard it helps."

As they stumbled around, Amore tripped a bit, catching himself on the counter top with his left hand. His right arm was still locked with Stevenson's. The move sandwiched the two together.

Suddenly it went silent. They were now face-to-face, with nobody else in sight. Stevenson grabbed the back of Amore's head and they began kissing. As drunk as Amore was – and he went on to black out several times from alcohol, after that night – he'd never forget a second of that night.

Amore closed his eyes and for a moment wasn't exactly sure where he was. Between the alcohol and now the kissing, these were experiences he hadn't yet dealt with - and certainly emotions he was yet to feel.

He was drunk and in love.

"Come on, let's just go lay down for a bit on the couch," Stevenson said.

"Oh, okay," Amore said, not quite sure what to say.

They sat down on the couch, but within minutes, passed out next to each other. What was supposed to be a brief reprieve from the party turned into nine hours of dreamless sleep.

"Amore, Amore! Wake up, man," Russell said, shaking the shoulder that didn't have Stevenson's head resting on it. "Come on! Coach is gonna kill us!"

Amore opened his eyes about a quarter of the way and was barely able to compose a thought, much less a sentence.

"What time is it?" he asked.

"It's after eight," Russell said. "We were supposed to be at practice 10 minutes ago already."

"Where are we?" he asked.

"At Lila's. You know – the girl on your shoulder!" Russell said, beginning to get a bit agitated.

"Oh... the party," Amore said. "So why are we still here?"

"You two came in here and passed out early and we kept on partying and all crashed on the floor," Russell explained. "But we have to go! You have those guys from Syracuse and Penn State. Coach is going to straight up kill us!"

"Oh, no!" Amore yelled, jumping up and spilling Stevenson to the other side of the couch.

Unable to get a word out in time, Stevenson just sat there, hair disheveled, as Russell and Amore raced out the door.

## Four:
## Hit the Field, Kid

Still wearing the same clothes from the night before, and with their teeth far from brushed, Russell and Amore hopped on their bikes and peddled feverishly.

"Not so fast," Amore said. "I think I'm going to..."

Suddenly, he screeched the brakes and jumped off his bike. As the bike crashed to its side, front wheel still spinning, he began vomiting on the side of the road.

"Oh, man," Russell said, stopping about 20 feet past where Amore was spewing.

"Okay, okay. I'm fine. Let's go," Amore said.

As they arrived at the school, the entire team was waiting outside the gym, yet to hit the practice field.

"Where in the hell have you boys been?" McBride asked, taking his hands from his hips and flailing them wildly in the air.

They stood there speechless. They couldn't so much as even mutter an excuse.

"Thomas Amore, let's go. I'll deal with your excuses later. You have two gentlemen here to meet you," McBride said as the team and two of its tardy partygoers stood there.

Still wearing khaki pants and a polo shirt, Amore at least somewhat looked the part.

As far as odor went, well... that was another story.

"You look good anyway, boy," McBride said. "You smell like a damn distillery, though. Why in the world did you let me down like this, boy?"

"Coach, I... I just," Amore attempted.

"You ain't got nothin' to say, boy!" McBride said.

As they walked into the coach's office, the two recruiters from Syracuse and Penn State stood up to greet them.

"Tom Johnson, Penn State," said a man wearing a dark blue sweat suit.

"This is our prized possession, Mr. Thomas Amore. Unfortunately, our boy was boozin' a bit last night, so never mind the smell of his great night on the town," McBride interrupted before allowing the now somewhat puzzled recruiters to shake both of their hands.

"Oh, okay. Well, let's just hope that was a one-off. I'm Michael Opera, with Syracuse," said a man dressed head-to-toe in blue and orange. "We would certainly like to bring you aboard, Thomas, as long as you can keep the whiskey to a minimum, get your math grade up, and keep up the hard work on the football field."

"And we at Penn State echo Mr. Opera's sentiments," Johnson said.

"I'll tell you what, gentlemen, let's get out there on the field so I can run some drills, seeing how as I'm already running behind schedule," McBride said. "Perhaps we can reconvene once I get a few drills out of the way. After that, I can let you guys dictate a few things you'd like to see from Thomas."

"Sounds great," Johnson said, looking toward Opera. "Good by you?"

"Yeah. That'd be fine," Opera said.

The four of them walked out together, initially, before McBride and Amore broke off, heading toward the locker room.

As they rounded the corner, McBride slapped Amore upside the head.

"Get your head on straight, kid. I'm extremely disappointed in you. I can't have you slugging around like a bum out there today. Well, actually, not any day; but especially not today. What the hell were you thinking?" McBride said.

Amore's lips moved a bit, but he just couldn't manage to get the words out.

"You know what, kid? I don't even want to hear it. Just get out there and work your butt off today," McBride said.

It was around 10 a.m. by the time they actually hit the field. The sun was pounding down; it would have taken a sword to cut through the humidity, with the temperature approaching 90. You could have bottled Amore's sweat and sold it as moonshine.

"First-team offense against second-team defense!" McBride yelled before blowing his whistle. "Line it up, boys!"

As Amore walked up to the formation, he fumbled around with buckling his chin strap. Higgins turned around and noticed he was acting uncharacteristically slow and disorganized.

"You all right, Amore?" he asked.

"Uh, yeah, let's go," he said, somewhat unsure.

Higgins turned, got under center, and began calling out his cadence.

"Blue 90, blue 90, set, go!" he barked.

The words sounded like slow motion to Amore. His heart was beating out of rhythm. His head was pounding. The alcohol-infused sweat was already pouring down into his eyes. The taste of whiskey still soured his mouth.

Blue 90 was a run play; but which gap, he wondered?

As he came up from behind Higgins, Amore's mind went blank. He couldn't remember which side he was supposed to go to once he got the ball.

As Higgins stuck the ball into Amore's chest, he panicked and crashed directly into him. The ball went flying out, Higgins fell backward and clueless as to where the ball was, and Amore stood there, only to get pile-driven into the ground by a bull-rushing defensive lineman.

McBride blew the whistle discontentedly.

"Again, again!" he yelled. "Line it up and run the same freakin' play."

Higgins walked up to the line. The linemen took their stance.

Amore was still trying to shake the cobwebs out from the big hit.

"Focus, Amore!" McBride yelled.

Amore knew not to look over. He simply bent his knees, put one hand on the ground, and looked dead ahead.

"Blue 90, blue 90, set, go!" Higgins again called.

The offensive and defensive lines let out a collective thump as they collided, and this time Amore took the ball smoothly but couldn't seem to find a gap. He tried to bounce it outside, relying on his speed, but was caught from behind by the defensive end.

"How in the world can that be, Amore?" McBride yelled from the sideline. "The fastest guy on the team gets caught by a defensive end?"

McBride joined the huddle the next time around.

"Okay, men... goal line formation. Power right, two hole," he explained. "Blast your way through, Amore. Blast your way right out of that hangover."

Amore planted his feet, bent down, and pushed his hands into the dry summer earth. His knuckles turned white as his fingers pressed down.

His body, still not in its typical highly conditioned form, trembled a bit – partly due to dehydration and in part due to his nerves for the poor showing.

"Red 47, red 47, set, go!" Higgins screamed out.

The offensive and defensive lines once again let off a collective thump. This time, the play call had Amore running directly into that very pile of humanity.

Higgins turned and jammed the ball into Amore's uneasy stomach.

Amore clenched his teeth, scrunched his cheeks, lowered his head, and ran like a locomotive – well, like a locomotive nearing the station, anyway. It was not his usual style of play; he was running out of pure desperation.

He barreled through the cluster of players but met an unsuspecting defender in the end zone – the ground.

The force with which Amore ran drove him through the pack but straight into the ground. He screamed in pure terror as things went from bad to worse.

"Coach!" he yelled, lying on his back, holding his right arm across his chest. "Coach, come here quick!"

The team stood silent while several players waved McBride over, knowing something was wrong.

"What is it, kid?" McBride asked.

"It's, it's... it's my arm, Coach," Amore said, struggling to get the words out. "I think it's broken."

The team's athletic trainer ran over. "Don't move," she said.

It was obvious that Amore's arm was badly broken. His forearm had a bend like a second wrist.

"We need to get you to the hospital," the trainer said. "Hold the underside of your forearm with your left hand and keep your right arm bent at the elbow."

As Amore walked off the field en route to the hospital, he passed the recruiters from Syracuse and Penn State. Both looked disappointed, standing with their arms crossed, shaking their heads.

"Too bad," one said.

Amore wasn't sure which one it was, so he turned and tried to plead his case.

"I can still do it. I promise, guys!" he yelled, now from a distance, with his head turned back. "Don't give up on me."

There was no response.

McBride turned practice over to his assistants and drove Amore to the hospital. As the door closed in his rusty 1952 Ford pickup truck, Amore knew what was coming next. To his surprise, however, it took longer than expected.

The two made it about five minutes without a word being exchanged.

Only the sound of the wind whistling through the truck's side vent windows broke what was otherwise silence. Amore looked over, and McBride knew he was looking, but still they remained speechless.

"Coach, you're mad at me, aren't you?" Amore asked, finally breaking the tension.

McBride looked over, opened his mouth as if he were about to say something, shook his head, and turned his focus back to the road ahead.

"Come on, Coach, say something," Amore begged, fighting back tears not only from the pain within his arm, but also from utter disappointment.

"Kid, it's just there ain't much to say. You really messed up. That's all there is to it," McBride said, not even looking in Amore's direction.

"Do you think I still have a chance with those guys?" Amore asked.

"Who, you mean the guys from Penn State and Syracuse?" McBride responded.

"Well... yeah," Amore said.

"No, kid. I don't think so at all. I think you had a wonderful chance and you flat out blew it. You decided that for whatever reason, last night was more important than an opportunity of a lifetime," McBride explained. "You show up reeking of booze, can't pull your head out of the clouds, and then break your arm running like a wild cowboy – and you expect these guys to be impressed?"

"Well, I just... I don't know, Coach," Amore said. "Maybe I'll get back out there this season and win them back over."

"I hate to break it to you, kid, but I'd say you are probably done playing football," McBride said in a surprisingly calm tone.

"What am I going to do, Coach?" Amore asked.

"Up until today, kiddo, I'd say there wasn't anything you couldn't do," a clearly disappointed McBride said. "I just can't believe it. I hope whatever led you down that path last night was worth it. If it was a woman, she better be the one. You just lost one dream, so I hope you at least found the girl of your dreams, assuming that's what made you act like a jerk. But guys will always act like idiots over women, so you don't even need to clarify that point."

"Sorry, Coach," Amore said, tears now slipping from his eyes. "Sorry."

McBride again shook his head, and they didn't exchange another word until they pulled into the hospital parking lot.

The rumble of the engine in McBride's pickup truck was similar to the feeling Amore had brewing in his stomach. As they pulled into a parking spot, Amore's previously slow stream of tears exploded into a gushing river.

"I think I'm going to be sick, Coach," he said as McBride pulled his brake up and shut the engine off.

"Goddamn it, boy. Pull it together!" a now red-faced, visibly angry McBride yelled. "This is called 'facing your consequences!' This is part of being a man! If you ever want to amount to anything, you'll quit whining, wipe those sorry tears from your face, and get ready to walk into that hospital like a man! A day ago you were the best football player in the area. Today you are squealing like a little girl who fell off her tricycle. Now, let's go!"

Amore knew better than to talk back. He reached over with his left hand – right arm still slumped across his lap – and opened the passenger door.

He walked toward the emergency room doors and did his best to dry his eyes and sniffle in the little bit of mucus that ran from his nose.

They walked into a chaotic scene in the emergency room. An elderly man, perhaps schizophrenic, screamed bloody murder; it appeared as though he had been beaten badly, with his nose oozing blood and several open wounds visible on his face.

Another woman wept in the corner, crying that her father had drunk himself to death.

Doctors consoled a family in the other corner, all of whom were crying.

In comparison, Amore's broken arm was but a hangnail.

"You don't have it so bad anymore, huh, kid?" McBride asked, in a subtle enough way that only Amore could make it out. "Look around this joint."

They checked in and prepared for what would be a long wait.

"You want a soda or something?" McBride asked.

"Yeah, Coach. Maybe a root beer, if that's okay," Amore responded in his softest tone.

"I'll get us both one," McBride said.

McBride came back over to a slumped over and dejected version of Amore. For the first time, the fierce coach with the powerful jaw saw his protégé, a teenage boy who he viewed as the son he'd never had, completely defeated.

The winner he once saw gallop at ease on the football field was suddenly sitting in the emergency room. Though he knew he shouldn't feel bad because "the boy," as he called Amore, had brought it on himself, he felt a fatherly need to inject something positive.

"Here, kid. Let's enjoy a soda," McBride said, placing one hand on Amore's shoulder and extending the can of root beer with the other.

"Sit up," McBride said calmly. "There's an important lesson you need to learn from this today."

"What's that, Coach?" Amore asked, correcting his posture.

"You and I both know that Penn State and Syracuse are both no longer options," McBride said. "Today marks the day you begin focusing on how you want to spend the rest of your life. We all learn from the mistakes we make in this life. And, unfortunately, God only gives us only one life to live, so when we do squander the chances he gives us, either they weren't meant to be, or we must own up to it and move on."

"Okay, Coach," Amore said, knowing his dreams had been dashed and reputation badly tarnished in just a day. "So, for sure, you think there's no chance at college football for me?"

"Well, boy, not with those programs. And I hate to say it, but I doubt you'll play at all this season. That arm is definitely broken," McBride continued.

Amore nodded his head in agreement and they sat there in silence for a moment.

"What if I were to get drafted?" Amore asked.

"What - you mean, like into the war?" McBride asked, referring to the ongoing situation in Vietnam.

"Yes. Maybe that could be how I turn this mess around, Coach," Amore said.

McBride smiled. You could tell he saw a little bit of the leader in Amore that he'd once seen on the football field.

"That would be admirable of you, boy, but quite dangerous," McBride said, patting him on the back.

"Well, Coach, if I can't play football, I don't know what else I would do to make my mark," Amore said.

"We'll see what happens," McBride said, taking a sip of his soda. "Let's just get you all fixed up here today and take it one step at a time."

"Okay, Coach," Amore said, nodding slowly.

"Amore?" a woman nurse called out, coming from behind a set of swinging doors. "Thomas Amore?"

"Right here," Amore said, raising his left hand, holding his right one across his chest as though it were already in a sling.

McBride got up behind him and the three of them walked into an exam room for the next series of questions.

"Well, I am guessing that, based on your attire, you hurt yourself playing football?" the nurse asked, pointing to Amore's football pants and cleats, which he'd never changed out of.

"Yes, ma'am," Amore said. "I hit the ground kind of hard and just felt a terrible pain."

"Oh, you boys and your football," the nurse said, rolling her eyes. "Where do you play?"

"Well, I did play at School 16," Amore said. "I bet no more, though, huh?"

"Let's get you an X-ray and find out," the nurse said.

It could have been the long wait and the talk with McBride, but the nurse seemed to have an additional calming effect on Amore. He was very easygoing about the whole process. And even when the nurse came back with the X-ray results, he didn't seem to have a worry one way or another.

"It's bad, isn't it, nurse?" he asked. "It's okay if it is. I know I need to move on."

"Well, that's an unusual response from a young man your age," the nurse said. "And yes, honey. It is bad. You shattered the growth plate in your wrist and have a subsequent break in your forearm. I am afraid you will have to be in a hard cast for the next four months."

"Okay. I understand," Amore said. "Definitely no football with the cast, right?"

"No. No football, honey," the nurse said with a chuckle.

As the nurse left, she asked that McBride leave the room while Amore had the cast put on.

Amore sat in the room alone for what seemed like an eternity; but in reality it was perhaps 30 minutes. Still, it was enough time that he sat and reflected on his recent decisions. He also thought quite a bit about Lila Stevenson and that maybe he had feelings for her. Like most teenagers, his imagination began running wild.

He thought to himself: *What if I volunteered to go to the war and came home a hero? Maybe, then, Lila and I could run off together and lead a nice life with a white picket fence – maybe even a dog.*

The doctor entered the room, interrupting Amore's thoughts.

"Mr. Amore?" he asked, chart and X-rays in hand.

"Yes, sir," Amore said.

Before he knew it, the now arm-in-cast Amore was walking out into the waiting room where McBride sat with his legs crossed, reading the newspaper. Next to him on the end table was collection of two more cans of soda he'd drunk while Amore was getting his cast on.

"Well, I guess this is the new me," Amore said, gesturing with his casted arm.

McBride lowered the paper, glanced at the boy, and chuckled.

"I guess so, kid," McBride said. "I guess so. Let's get you back home to your mother. She's worried sick about you."

"Oh, God," Amore said. "Did you talk to her?"

"Yes. I called her when you were in there," McBride explained. "She told me she hadn't seen you since last night. To avoid a scene or making it any worse on you, I made up a little fib. I said the team stayed at my place."

"You didn't have to do that, Coach," Amore said. "I don't deserve it."

"Forget it. Just don't act like a jackass ever again," McBride clarified.

It was dark outside as they drove home with the more tolerable summer air blowing through McBride's beat-up old truck.

It had been quite the day. But once the sun had retired in the west, one couldn't help but laugh. So it was that McBride – the guy he viewed as a father – and Amore did just that: they laughed.

Perhaps it was the tamer air that blew the sense of frustration, anger, and outright disappointment right off them as they drove home that night. Perhaps it was just the experience of defeat and learning a lesson, especially given their mentor-protégé relationship. Or, perhaps it was simply a matter of being human and owning up to the fact that error is part of existence.

Regardless, as they pulled into Amore's driveway, leaving his bike behind at the school for obvious reasons, McBride cut the laughter short.

"Okay, boy," McBride said, face turned solemn. "I was serious about what I said earlier. Today is the day you decide to become a man. You need to understand what it takes in the future. I've always known you to be a man among boys, and I expect the same to carry over into everything you do in life."

"I know, Coach," Amore said.

Amore paused and looked out the window. He wanted to reach his right arm out and feel the innocence of the summer air, but looking down at his right arm - the closest to the window – it simply wasn't possible.

"I see what I've done here, Coach," Amore said. "I know I can do better. I just know it."

"Okay, boy," McBride said, reaching his right hand out to Amore's left shoulder to console him. "Aside from the obvious, which is that I expect you at every team function the rest of the year, I want you to do another thing for me."

"What's that, Coach?" Amore asked.

"You need to be the best son you can be to your mother," McBride said.

"She needs you, kid. I don't know much about ladies; trust me on that," he continued. "But I do know that if you are going to be the man I think you can be – one who overcomes a day like today and becomes a champion – you can't do it without a woman in your life. Especially your mother. A true man will always treat women with the utmost respect."

"How do you know about my mom and I, Coach?" Amore asked with a sad ring to his voice.

"I was born at night, but it wasn't last night, kid. And don't forget that I've been around your family for quite some time now," McBride said. "Now go in there and use that one arm of yours to turn over a new leaf."

"Okay, Coach," Amore said. "I like that - 'Use that one arm of yours to turn over a new leaf.' I'm going to do just that, Coach. I promise."

Amore reached over to let himself out, but he did so with his right arm – already forgetting that is was mummified. He let out a screeching groan, followed by a lengthy sigh.

McBride would have none of Amore's pity party.

"Boy, look at me," McBride said, forcefully. "What did I tell you?"

Amore looked over, but couldn't see directly into his face. The streetlight behind him was blinding, but still McBride's strong jaw cut the light; and that's all Amore needed to see to know he meant business.

"I know. I know," Amore said. "Today I become a man, Coach. I got this."

"All right, boy," McBride said. "I believe in you."

This time, Amore reached over with his left hand and slowly let himself out of the truck. He was tired beyond belief. Aside from battling his first hangover, he had spent the entire day in the slow-moving emergency room. It was a day filled with sights, sounds, and emotions he had yet to feel. For better or worse, it had been the longest day of his young life.

Amore walked up the driveway slowly, picking his borderline-rancid t-shirt off his chest. His clothes – football pants still bearing pads – may as well have been glued on, by that point.

As he made his way to the front steps, the porch light turned on and the door opened. His mother stood there and the two awkwardly stared at each other through the screen door.

"Well, Thomas," she said, breaking the pause.

"Sorry about last night, Mom," he said.

"Coach McBride told me that he had all you guys over, and that's fine and well. I just wish you would have told me about it and not stormed out," she said, arms crossed.

"You were drunk," Thomas responded.

She opened the screen door and waved in her only son. Hardly a second later, she slapped him across the face.

"How dare you question whether or not I was drunk," she said, an angry tear spilling down her cheek. "You are a 17-year-old boy! I am an adult. If I want to have a drink or two, I will; and you are not to tell me one way or the other! Are we understood?"

*Think of Coach*, Thomas thought. *Think of Coach. Become the man. Patch things up. Become the man.*

He knew that his behavior was wrong, and he wanted desperately to hold in his emotions. But that's what he had always done amid his mother's angry, drunken rants. And so the water finally boiled over the top.

"I hate you!" Thomas screamed, deviating from his thought process. "You're nothing but a selfish drunk!"

She again slapped him, this time forcing his lip into his teeth and drawing blood.

He stood there, rage building inside. He tasted the salty blood in his mouth and reached up with his left hand to check just how much there was.

Looking down at his blood-coated fingers, he was ready to blow a gasket. If he were a tea kettle, steam would have been escaping quickly while the whistle screamed ferociously.

Still, he stood there. He looked up and stared directly into her typically-glazed eyes. His head began to shake a bit out of trepidation while his eyes became squinty and his cheeks and nose crunched in.

"You're scaring me, Thomas!" she said.

"I'm scaring you?" he asked, eyes gone crazy. "Scaring you? You have got to be kidding me! You know what's scary? Not having a father and having a mother who is a train-wreck drunk!"

And with that, he blew past her and stormed back to his room.

Unlike his last trip there, there was no playful bounce to his step – no pretending to elude a defender. Despite still being in football cleats, this was all business.

He got to his room and began peeling his shirt off. This was no easy task with a broken wing. He winced in pain, but managed to get it off. He kicked his cleats in separate directions, unleashing a foul odor from his days-old socks.

Once again he let out a sigh.

On his wall was a poster of his favorite football player: Cookie Gilchrist of the AFL's Buffalo Bills.

He stood there, bleeding from his lip, and looked at the poster.

Again he sighed.

Then his heart began pounding. His left eye twitched. The feeling of rage had taken over.

He charged the poster and threw a haymaker punch with his able hand directly through his hero, penetrating the wall behind it.

With one more swipe, he ripped the poster off the wall and wildly threw it aside. Bits of crumbling plaster fell to the floor.

All he'd ever wanted was to be a professional football player. The reality of the vicious last 24 hours had finally set in.

Despite being as tired as a first-time hangover makes a person, he hardly slept a wink that night. He tossed and turned, writhing in pain when he rolled on to his right arm.

Amore spent the night on his back, tears trickling out of his eyes as the pain beyond his arm finally set in. He desperately missed his father and was now equally missing the woman that he'd previously known as his mother. And now, because of his own missteps, he was questioning his future.

Given his battle with sleep that night, the alarm clock may as well have been a fire truck racing through his room. It was loud, obnoxious, and startled the pants off of him. Just as he had finally gotten a minute of pain-free quietness, the alarm howled – signaling that it was time to face the harsh realities of his destruction.

"Good grief, enough!" he grumbled to himself as the alarm rattled his brain.

Amore rolled over and clubbed the irritating clock off the nightstand with his casted arm.

Not only was it the morning after a day from hell, but it was the last day of summer vacation – not exactly an ending fit for a fairytale.

As he sat up and planted his feet on the floor, he looked at his path of destruction from the night before. The Gilchrist poster was belly-up on the floor with a gaping hole that might as well have screamed, "Look what you've done, you maniac."

The plaster wall on which the poster had once hung didn't seem to have fixed itself, either.

"What a mess. Pull it together, Thomas," he said to himself.

As he stood up, the stench from his now-48-hour-old boxer shorts sent an uppercut to his nostrils.

Athletes often make reference to a lucky pair of drawers. For Thomas Amore, the pair that clung to his thighs that morning were anything but those of good fortune, so he scraped them off and waltzed down the hallway – completely naked – on the path to a much-needed shower. He didn't care if the blinds were open and especially not if his mother was there to notice.

As the shower water hit him, it was as though the cleansing had a whole new meaning. He stood in there for an hour, pondering his thoughts while the water ricocheted off his expressionless face. All the while, his casted arm hung free outside the curtain.

This, of course, made for a watery mess outside of the tub – one that, under ordinary circumstances, he would have certainly taken the time to soak up.

But the start to his day was far from typical.

As he reached out of the tub with his left arm to grab a towel, he noticed the small pond he had created. He scrunched his brow for a moment, briefly contemplating drying up the excess water. Hardly a second later, he let out a very non-concerned "eh" and continued on his way.

With no sign of his mother, Amore walked out the front door looking and feeling like a new man.

Humming "I Want to Hold Your Hand" by The Beatles, he began walking.

With no particular destination in mind, he ended up in the park, where he found a bench with a great view of a manmade lake. The sights and sounds of the Frederick Law Olmsted-designed park were quite therapeutic, a fact Amore had learned by running its trails when training for football.

No sounds of the city – and, more importantly, no sounds of a nagging mother. The birds were chirping in conversational fluctuation. The soft wind blew on the peacefully rustling high grass closer to the water.

On the other side of the lake, a man and boy – likely father and son – were skipping rocks off the waveless water. Watching them, Thomas Amore felt at peace.

He thought about Lila Stevenson. He thought about becoming a hero in the war. He thought that maybe one day they could have children of their own, and he could be skipping rocks with his son.

*Life wasn't so bad after all*, he thought. He just needed a second chance.

## FIVE:

## WITH A LITTLE HELP FROM A FRIEND

Clad in his signature outfit – white tennis sneakers with tube socks, short-in-length athletic shorts, and a tight-fit polo shirt – McBride paced his 10-foot-by-12-foot office, contemplating whether or not to call an old friend.

His old friend was Colonel James Thompson, a recruiter at the United States Military Academy at West Point (also known as the Army).

Thompson, McBride thought, might be just the guy to give Amore the second chance he needed. He could not only play football for a highly respected collegiate program, but he could also serve his country in the years that followed.

And he paced. Back and forth. Back and forth. Finally, words from a poster on his wall made the decision a no-brainer.

"There is no I in team," he said to himself, looking at the poster.

"The kid probably can't do it on his own."

McBride took a seat at his desk and flipped through a Rolodex of business cards.

"Q, R, S," he said, flipping through alphabetical tabs. "T... Thompson."

He pulled Thompson's card from the mix and spun the numbers through the rotary telephone atop his worn-down metal desk.

Ring... ring... ring...

"West Point. This is Thompson."

"Thompson! Bill McBride here," he said. "Long time no talk, my friend."

"McBride, you son of a gun!" Thompson said. "How the heck are ya?"

"Well..." McBride said, letting out a sigh. "I wish I was calling to shoot the breeze and not with something of an exploratory question and possible favor to ask."

"That's all right, Bill," Thompson said. "What's on your mind?"

McBride told Thompson a story about a young man who had a lot going for him – an all-Western New York athlete who also excelled in the classroom. But McBride, who was nothing if not transparent, didn't sugarcoat things.

"Listen, Thompson," he said. "This is also a kid who needs a good firm boot to the rear – especially after what he just pulled."

"Huh?" Thompson asked, after hearing a mostly-rosy tale about Amore.

"Well," McBride said. "Here's the short of it: The kid hasn't had a father figure other than me, and I hardly qualify. His old man passed away years ago, and, well... I think maybe he's starting to act out a bit. The kid's not been in any trouble until just recently, when he did something you and I did more times than we'd like to admit: He got a little boozy at a party with a bunch of cheerleaders."

Thompson laughed.

"So what are you telling me?" Thompson asked. "Did he get into a drunken tussle or something?"

"No," McBride said. "He showed up to practice hung over and absolutely blew his opportunity with Penn State and Syracuse."

"But only that one time?" Thompson asked.

"Yes," McBride said. "And full disclosure: He also broke his wrist at that practice. But he'll be fine. As of right now, he thinks his days of playing ball are over. It may have been his emotions talking – or maybe still the booze – but he said he plans to enlist."

"What did you say his grades look like, again?" Thompson asked.

"He's been an honor student each of his three years, despite only mediocre grades in math," McBride said.

"Okay – and just as important: What has the kid done on the football field? If he's willing to join the academy, I'm sure Coach would love to have him on the football team," Thompson said. "Heck... if the kid's that good, I'm sure Coach already knows all about him. Buffalo's only a few hours away, and you know how word travels."

"He's 6-foot-2, 190 pounds, and picked up more than 1,400 yards as our running back," McBride said. "And I tell you what, Thompson – he could play anywhere on the field. Furthermore, I imagine he'd make an exceptional soldier."

Pondering his next move, Thompson tapped his fingers on his heavily lacquered oak desk and gazed around his office, which featured a large American flag on the wall and a bookcase full of awards from his years of service.

"Sounds like an all-American boy to me," Thompson said. "Let's arrange to bring him in for a visit, if he's interested."

"You won't regret it," McBride said.

And regret it, Thompson and the football team's coaching staff would not. Amore immediately fell in love with all things United States Military Academy at West Point and vice versa.

# Six:
## Oh, To Be in College Again

**W**hen it came to his collegiate career, the numbers don't lie.

His 3,439 career rushing yards still ranked Amore fifth on Army's all-time rushing list – despite not playing as a freshman, per the academy's rules back then. During his senior year alone, he ran for 1,231 yards – including a 267-yard single-game performance that is still discussed today.

As one of its all-time great athletes, the name Thomas Amore became something of legendary status at West Point. But Amore often cringed when his personal accolades were brought up, because he believed the two most important numbers were 23 and seven – the remarkable win-loss record for his graduating class of 1969.

His four years – three as a player – at West Point were among the most storied in the long history of the academy.

Those four years also rank among the most memorable for matters beyond football. Every cadet, Amore included, was cognizant of the ongoing situation in Vietnam, and that certainly made life at West Point equal parts anxious and heartbreaking.

When Amore arrived as a trainee in 1966, that graduating class lost more men in Vietnam than any other. As time went on, Amore and his teammates and classmates would hear the names of those who'd been lost, including some who they'd come to know. Amore and his fellow trainees – known as plebes – would never admit to feeling fear, but there was a definite sense of sadness in the air.

The spring of 1966 was nothing if not confusing for the football team. Less than two weeks before spring practice was scheduled to get underway, Paul Dietzel resigned as head coach – a sudden move that left Amore nervous about his own future.

Candidate after candidate, it seemed, turned down the academy's offer to fill Dietzel's shoes. Amore tried not to let that situation bother him and continued working hard as spring practice moved forward without a head coach in place.

Luckily for Amore, it turned out that the next head coach was already on the field during those initial practices. Tom Cahill, who was a member of the team's coaching staff, was named head coach – and he instantly took a liking to Amore.

Cahill, of course, was later widely recognized as having an eye for talent. The coaching staff that he assembled included the likes of Bill Parcells, who went on to become a Super Bowl-winning head coach in the National Football League.

As a sophomore, Cahill named Amore as the team's starting running back on a team that surprised most of the country by going 8-2.

Amore paved the way by averaging 5.1 yards per rushing attempt.

The following season, the Cadets' only loss in their first nine games came on account of an inexplicable pass interference call on what would have been a game-winning touchdown. What appeared to be a 14-10 win became a 10-7 loss.

The loss was hardly devastating, though, as the Cadets cruised past every other opponent in the weeks that followed, which included Army's first-ever trip to Colorado Springs to take on the Air Force. In fact, with an 8-1 record, the team was invited to play in the Sugar Bowl.

Amore had dreams of his team shining in the big game. Unfortunately, the Pentagon imagined it differently.

Among other reasons, government officials were concerned that sending the Cadets football team to New Orleans, the host city of that year's Sugar Bowl, would send the wrong message to those who were serving the U.S. in Vietnam. And so, by order of the Pentagon, Army had to decline the offer.

Keep in mind that this was 1967. Things were quite different than today, when members of the military are respected by most Americans.

Given the widespread protest of the Vietnam War, the government was reluctant to shine the spotlight on the Army football team – a point that increasingly bothered Amore, who was also coping with the death of his mother.

Perhaps to prove what an extraordinary athlete he was – but more likely to suppress the pain of the loss of his mother, who passed away earlier that year – Amore went out for lacrosse as a junior and became an All-American, leading the Army in scoring. Incredibly, he had never picked up a lacrosse stick until college.

After graduation in 1969, Amore was sent to Vietnam to serve in the 8th Infantry Division and then was called back to West Point in 1972 because the coaching staff – and even Thompson, his first supporter at the academy – thought he could help with recruiting efforts.

But by the time he returned to join his former coaches, he was a shell of the man who'd barreled through defenders as a football player. He was timid – soft, even – and had very little passion for much that didn't involve drowning his sorrows.

And after just two days on the job, it was obvious to him and everyone around him that football wasn't helping Amore cope with his post-Vietnam struggles.

Thomas Amore left the academy behind and returned to Buffalo – uninspired and broken down, physically and emotionally.

July 22, 1969

Status: Not delivered

*Dear Lila:*

*If I sent this letter, there's a good chance I am in big trouble. Whether it be with my superiors or simply my mental/physical state – that is anyone's guess. I'm going to fight with everything I've got to be strong and to hold this letter in my personal box.*

*But the long and short of it is this: I need to get out of here – as soon as yesterday. I need to come home; I simply don't know how much more I can take. My nights are sleepless, with my nerves on constant edge and my mind constantly thinking of you.*

*If you do get this letter, please know that I will get better. Please – I'm begging you in advance – give me a chance to heel, and everything will be just fine. I will be just fine. More importantly: We will be just fine.*

## For the Love of Thomas Amore

*If I'm to be on my way home, I will need you more than ever. Still, part of me hopes you never have to read this letter; that will have meant that I overcame whatever it is that is ailing me. Nevertheless, should you read this – it comes with love. Always with love.*

*--Thomas*

## SEVEN:
## ON THE SHORES OF LAKE ERIE

It was an ordinary start to the morning for Dr. Preston Peterson.

The sun nonchalantly poked through the 12-foot crowning windows amid the sprawling landscape of his lavish bedroom.

After getting out of bed, he casually slid his feet into a pair of nearby slippers and made his way down a wide set of heavily lacquered stairs.

Once at the bottom, he proceeded down a long hallway – donning acclaim for his research, the dozen-or-so best-selling books he had written, and most notably, his Nobel Peace Prize – toward the smell of fresh coffee in the kitchen.

Preston's wife, Irene, sat at the kitchen table, staring out the window at the frigid waves crashing onto their backyard beach.

"It's getting really nasty out there, Preston," she said. "And it's probably only going to get worse, considering the lake isn't frozen yet."

"I see that," he said, filling up a coffee mug. "I really wish I didn't have to speak at this event today. I'd probably just take the day off."

"You should take the day off," Irene said. "You're constantly working."

The howling wind, sending snow in every direction, rattled the far-from-rickety windows of the Petersons' 6,000-square-foot mansion along the shores of Lake Erie.

"I know," he said, taking a sip of his coffee with his brow scrunched. "I have to, though."

"Why?" Irene asked. "The house is paid for. The Mercedes in the garage is paid for."

"I know," he said, this time growing a bit frustrated. "But the house, cars, and everything else we've done over the years never would have been paid for if that was my approach to work."

"Oh, Preston, come on," she pleaded. "Just take a step back, for once. For years and years, it's been just work, work, work. Can't you just enjoy the fruits of your labor? I can't take this much longer!"

"Not today, Irene," he said. "I've put too much into my work to not give some back. Speaking at these seminars does just that. Not to mention, I've got plenty of work to get to before I head to the speaking engagement."

Typically, the Petersons stuck to a methodical breakfast routine. Preston would eat a bowl of oatmeal and a banana and drank two cups of coffee; Irene had two egg whites and rye toast along with a cup of tea.

They usually discussed myriad topics, especially the day ahead. But on this morning, conversation was sparse.

"Where will you be speaking?" Irene asked, breaking a prolonged silence (aside from the activity outside).

"Downtown," he said quietly.

"So you are going to drive all the way to the northernmost point in the city – in this awful weather – just to drive back to the other end of the city?" she asked.

"Yes," he said.

"Won't you at least take the train from your office to downtown? It's right there, after all," she pleaded.

"Okay," he said, keeping true to his one-word responses.

On paper, the Petersons had it all – money, modest fame, and a waterfront property. But work – or the relentless pursuit of it – had been a frequent point of contention through the years.

Despite his success, Dr. Peterson never felt content. Something was missing, and he never could quite pinpoint what was driving that unsettling feeling.

# Eight:
## The Other Side of the Tracks

Guys like Dr. Peterson – wealthy enough for two lifetimes – were seldom among the middle-class riders of Buffalo's Metro Rail, a train system that runs several miles along Main Street. Given the lousy weather and the train's relative convenience, he became the exception.

The train was maybe half-full, with an equal mix of college students and business people traveling from the northernmost point of the city to downtown.

Frozen to the core, Amore needed warmth – and sooner before later. Desperate for cover, he waited for the train to arrive at the fare-free stop. At the very least, he figured, he could avoid the wind for a little while by traveling – even if he had nowhere to be.

It was at that point that two men nearly of equal age – but at entirely different places in life – were seated across from one another.

Amore, sniffling and continuously wiping his runny nose, sat with his head down. His blood-stained beard gave him the look of a wild animal fresh off a feeding.

Wearing a long overcoat, a top hat, ear muffs and gloves, Dr. Peterson did his best to avoid eye contact. He looked at the floor, upon which

two murky saltwater streams flowed between the two of them, the after-
math of melting snow from the bottoms of each of their shoes. The two
bodies of water eventually collided, spreading side by side in the floor's
vertical grooves as the train left the station.

Dr. Peterson's eyes soon after drifted slowly upstream, narrowing in
on Amore's boots – the material of which was hardly distinguishable.

Seconds later, Dr. Peterson looked up, and the two were suddenly in
a non-confrontational staring contest.

Questioning everything was what had paved the road to success for
Dr. Peterson. So naturally, he had to inquire about Amore's appearance.

"Are you okay?" Dr. Peterson asked, blinking a few times while
scrunching his brow.

He expected Amore to lash out in an intoxicated rage, so Dr. Peterson cut in before an answer could be delivered.

"Well, I mean, rather, can I help you?" he asked.

"No," Amore said softly.

"No, you are not okay, or no I can't help you?" Dr. Peterson responded.

"Frankly, sir, I believe we both know that I'm not well," Amore said,
with a sobering ring to his voice. "And as for helping me... well, I don't
know what you expect to accomplish on this train ride."

And just like that, a switch flipped for Dr. Peterson who, especially
in his younger years, challenged everything. Homelessness, though – or
the road to homelessness – was a topic that Dr. Peterson had often pondered but he'd never dedicated any time to researching.

"Can I ask you something?" said Dr. Peterson, his curiosity and level of interest in Amore increasing by the second.

"Seems as though you just did," Amore said, smirking innocently from behind his gruff beard.

"Fair enough," Dr. Peterson said, chuckling. "Okay, well, I suppose I should start by introducing myself. My name is Preston Peterson. What is your name?"

"Nice to meet you, Dr. Peterson," Amore said. "I'm familiar with your work. My name is Tom Amore."

Amore extended his hand, but quickly withdrew it.

"Sorry," he said. "You probably don't want any part of touching my hand before it's washed."

Without hesitation, Dr. Peterson extended his hand.

"May I buy you a cup of coffee?" Dr. Peterson asked.

Amore blinked and clenched his lips a bit, as though in deep thought.

"I don't want to trouble you, Doctor," he said.

"Come on. We'll get off at the next stop. I know a place," Dr. Peterson said.

"Lafayette stop!" said the train conductor, moments later.

Outside, the wind – screaming between the buildings in downtown Buffalo – was anything but still, rifling snow in every direction. Visibility was limited at best.

"Come on, Tom," Dr. Peterson insisted. "Please join me."

It was such balance between curiosity and persistence that had carried Dr. Peterson throughout his life.

"Are you sure I'm not keeping you from something, Doctor?" Amore asked.

Dr. Peterson opened his mouth as if he had something to say, but instead briefly shook his head from side to side.

"Nothing I can think of," said Dr. Peterson, replaying in his head the cat-and-dog fight that he'd had with his wife.

The two battled through the stormy weather, Amore walking with a steady limp a step behind Dr. Peterson, who struggled to hold his hat to the top of his head. Dr. Peterson opened the door to a business, turning to usher Amore into the warm coffee shop.

There was just one problem: Amore had set off on a different route. He began veering back toward the train.

"Mr. Amore!" Dr. Peterson yelled, shuffling through the snow to catch him and gently grabbing his shoulder. "Please, Mr. Amore."

"Why do you care?" Amore asked. "What's in it for you, Doctor?"

"Coffee will do you well. It will do us both well," Dr. Peterson said.

Amore paced in the face of the howling, blustery wind.

"Well, I suppose a conversation with a bit of substance could do me well, anyhow," Amore said, hunched over to keep his stance.

Before long, the two were sitting across from each other, each with a cup of black coffee.

"So..." Dr. Peterson said, taking a sip of coffee. "How did this all happen?"

"Well," Amore said, clenching his coffee mug with both hands. "It's a long story - presuming you are asking beyond my appearance today."

"Please, Tom. Tell me the whole story," Dr. Peterson said.

May 20, 1969


Dearest Tom:

It's been two weeks since you've been gone, but it feels like two decades.

I've walked around the lake every morning, but it doesn't feel right without you. The spring flowers don't quite smell as fresh. The sun's sparkle off the water isn't as magnificent. And the birds' chirping doesn't seem as musical.

I hope whatever you're doing at this very moment, you can find time to imagine yourself at the lake – with me by your side. The good Lord knows that I've imagined you at my side.

If you can't tell, I am really struggling today. I knew that writing to you – even just a few paragraphs – would be cathartic. And I'm happy to say that it's slowly bringing a smile to my face.

You are such a strong guy, so I know I don't have to worry about you. But if you're struggling at all, please keep my letters near and dear, so that I'm always by your side.


Love always,
Lila

# NINE:
## MORE COFFEE, PLEASE

It's been said that the key to being an effective communicator is to be an excellent listener. Dr. Peterson certainly didn't need a reminder. He absorbed Amore's life story in just a matter of two hours.

Dr. Peterson was masterfully patient, with a mind both imaginative and incredibly retentive.

"I'm just about out of coffee," Dr. Peterson said, politely interrupting Amore's story. "Will you have another cup?"

"If you don't mind," Amore said. "Are you sure you have the time, Doctor?"

"My schedule is completely clear," Dr. Peterson said, glancing briefly at his watch and realizing he was already late for his commitment. "We should get a bite to eat, too. I have a feeling we could be here a while. How about a couple of breakfast sandwiches?"

Dr. Peterson's voice was one of little fluctuation, but not to be confused as being monotone and dull. His voice had a power over people – a calming, convincing rhythm that broadcast intelligence.

"Okay," Amore said. "I suppose I could eat. And it's truly nice to have someone to talk to at length, for once. It's been a while."

## TEN:

## LOVE IN A BOX

As Dr. Peterson and Amore neared the end of coffee number two, the barista stopped over to break a bit of news.

"Gentlemen, I just wanted to let you know that we are pretty much trapped here for the time being. The mayor just issued a travel ban, due to the weather. From what I hear, it's so bad that the train is trapped underground – with people in it," she said. "My manager said to take care of anyone who is stuck here. So as long as we are here, I will make sure we all eat. Hopefully we don't lose power."

Suddenly, all things became equal. Dr. Peterson, who always seemed to be on a strict schedule, was on Mother Nature's watch – a concept all too familiar to the homeless Amore.

"Well, I guess we're going to get to the bottom of your story after all, huh, Tom?" Dr. Peterson said, taking a last remaining lukewarm sip of coffee.

Amore nodded, glancing toward the frosted-over window.

"What do you know about love, Doc?" he asked, rather out of the blue.

"Well, that's a rather loaded question, wouldn't you say?" Dr. Peterson said, chuckling.

"Okay. More specifically, do you think it is love that keeps us going?" Amore asked. "I mean, like on days like today, when it seems like God has decided we are no longer a part of his plan. Do you think that by having even just a little bit of love in your heart – even just a flickering bulb – that it can be enough to get you through?"

"That's awfully deep, Tom," Dr. Peterson said, fumbling with his silverware a bit. "The thing about love, you see... it's just... it's very complex, I believe."

Dr. Peterson seemed to be getting unusually uncomfortable.

"Actually, you know what, Tom? I'm a jerk – an utter jerk. I've denied myself of love almost all of my life," he admitted. "Just this morning, I battled with my wife, who wanted nothing more than for me to stay home – you know, to spend the day with her - and not only that, but because she was concerned for my well-being with this weather. But instead, I just had to go to work. I'm 66 years old, Tom. And here I am."

The electricity in the coffee shop began to flicker while the switch seemed to flip between interviewee and interviewer with Amore and Dr. Peterson.

"That's probably rather typical in your line of work, no?" Amore asked. "I've always wondered how a guy in your position... you know: the published works, the Nobel Peace Prize for crying out loud... I've always wondered how you sleep at night. Where is there time? And what about your wife? How could you even maintain any sort of real connection?"

"I... I don't know as much as I think, I suppose, Tom," Dr. Peterson said. "It's just, well, you know – you've got to keep plugging away at work.

That Nobel Peace Prize didn't win itself."

Amore smirked a bit at Dr. Peterson's suggestion that he could relate to this idea.

"Well, actually, as you can probably surmise from my appearance, I really don't know what that's like," Amore said, chuckling. "But I hear what you're saying."

"Duly noted," Dr. Peterson said with a laugh.

"You know, Doc, sometimes I think the only thing that has kept me alive this long is this box that I carry," Amore said, plopping his wooden box on the table. "When I was in Vietnam, the love of my life, Lila, would write me at least once a week. She could say almost anything and it would lift my spirits – because it was her saying it. Even the sight of her perfectly penned cursive made my heart flutter – and it still does today."

"That's remarkable, Tom," Dr. Peterson said. "What else is in that box?"

"Mostly just love letters, along with a few others who wrote me during that time," Amore said. "The love letters, of course, were all from Lila. Throughout college and especially in the months leading up to me leaving for the war, we fell deeply in love. Our love made me forget about everything else in my life that crumbled at the time, including my relationship with my mother… the blown opportunity to play ball at Syracuse or Penn State. But finding love seemed to cure everything.

"Once I left for Vietnam, we kept in close contact by letter-writing, often discussing our future together – you know, getting married and starting a family and such."

"That's incredible," Dr. Peterson said. "And you've carried them all this time? How have you not lost them?"

"Sure have," Amore said. "That little bit of love that remains in my heart is what keeps me going sometimes. It's my cup of morning coffee, if you will. I have nothing else in this world, other than a little bit of love. There's no way I could ever let this box out of my grasp. To me, it's not always about happiness in the present tense these days; these letters help me recall a time in my life when the sun always shined."

"Wow. Where is Lola today, if you don't mind me asking?" Dr. Peterson inquired.

"Lila," Amore said, immediately correcting the uncharacteristically flustered Dr. Peterson.

Amore opened the box, thumbing through his collection.

"Here it is," he said. "Santa Fe, New Mexico, as of July 22, 1994."

"You two haven't spoken since?" Dr. Peterson asked.

"No, sir," Amore said. "Those were some dark times for me. I was drinking heavily and never really could fully shake Vietnam. Flashbacks were frequent, and I became known as something of an oddball. I tried like crazy to hold a job, but I just did not fit in. Well, at least I think I tried, anyway. Again – my mind was a bit... shall we say... polluted."

"So what happened? Did she quite literally write you off in that last letter?" Dr. Peterson asked, with growing intrigue in his voice.

Letting out a deep sigh, Amore opened his mouth to speak but seemed to be tongue-tied.

"Basically," Amore said. "Despite all of our contact over the years, I was too delusional to realize that she had moved on – until I received a letter that really clearly spelled it out: 'I'm married with children.' I penned a response to that note but was too ashamed to send it.

"Once I was sober – clean of all substances for a solid month – I re-read almost every letter... it was really quite sad. I don't know how I didn't interpret the changing tone and sometimes brutal honesty in her notes. I guess it could be that I was too inebriated to understand. After all, even in those days, letter-writing was our only means of communication. I didn't have a phone in my various residences, so she usually just sent letters once I was back from the war and occasionally in the years that followed.

"I never felt resentment for her, though. I knew it was me who sank the ship. There was love in every one of her words, Doc. But like you are saying, I was a much worse version of myself – a drunken, drug-using, self-absorbed failure."

"I'm still amazed that you've managed to keep those letters all this time," Dr. Peterson said.

"Well, Doc," Amore said. "I guess there's a lesson here for you. Your drug of choice is just a bit different. I made some poor choices even after I was given a second chance. But life doesn't always give you a third chance... or a 33rd, in my case."

Dr. Peterson sat there for a moment, nodding his head in agreement, but all the while with a puzzled look on his face. It was as though his finely tuned scientific brain finally came across an unfamiliar potion – and maybe, just maybe, things were finally coming into focus, as a result.

For years, Dr. Peterson lamented – often to his wife – that his life's work was incomplete. Millions of dollars, country club memberships and even a Nobel Peace Prize... none of it brought the long-term satisfaction that he imagined. But at that moment, Dr. Peterson had an epiphany: For years, he had surrounded himself with "yes men" people who padded his ego, and very few who had the courage to live in the moment.

And so there he was, accepting advice from a homeless stranger – and things never seemed clearer.

"I wish to heaven I could see what I wrote to her," Amore said. "Because I know for fact that in my mind, I always thought I'd get her back. So I can only imagine that my notes to her were either drunkenly poetic in some way – or they were desperate-sounding, literary abominations. There's no taking that stuff back, Doc. You can't erase ink."

Dr. Peterson smiled a bit, nodding his head.

"Right," he said. "You cannot take back what has been said in ink. That's why contracts are signed in ink, my friend."

Those last two words caught Amore off guard, and he let out a bit of laughter as a result.

"My friend," he said. "Are we friends, Doc?"

"We're friends," Dr. Peterson said. "You might be the most honest person I've ever met, Tom."

*July 22, 1994*

*Tom:*

*It breaks my heart when I read your sporadic letters.*

*I really wish you'd get the help you need. There are groups that work with veterans – and clearly you are in desperate need of such help. Drugs and alcohol will never help you overcome whatever happened to you overseas, but perhaps trained professionals can get you back to the man you*

<u>were</u>. *(I know that guy is still inside of you!)*

*I don't know how many ways or times I can tell you this, but I am married and have children now. I am happy with the life that I have created out here in Santa Fe. I truly wish you could find the same level of happiness.*

*The love you and I shared was beautiful, and it is something I will always hold in my heart. But out of respect for my family, I have to cease communicating with you.*

*I will say a prayer that this letter finds you well and that you find your way back to a sense of peace.*

*Take care,*

*Lila*

## Eleven:
## The Point of No Return

More than two feet of snow accumulated outside, according to a weather report on a nearby television. The entire region was completely locked down by a travel ban, the report continued.

"You know what," Dr. Peterson said, glancing at the television. "I don't mean to cut you off, but I'd better call my wife."

Dr. Peterson stepped away from the table to make his phone call.

Amore skimmed a newspaper that was sitting on top of their table while picking up bits and pieces of Dr. Peterson's call.

Dr. Peterson walked back to the table less than two minutes later with his eyebrows scrunched in discontent.

"I just wanted to tell her what was going on," he said. "And she jumped down my throat. When I told her that I wasn't coming home, she said I shouldn't bother, anyway. She just kept saying she told me not to leave – and the reality is... she's right."

"Well, doc," Amore said. "I hate to even suggest this, but it's just, well... never mind."

"What is it, Tom?" Dr. Peterson asked.

"Well, you know how sometimes you just know you screwed up?"

Amore asked. "And I mean REALLY screwed up. Like – it's not okay. The kind of mess in which you know it and everyone else knows that you know, but it's too late; the damage is done, man. The kind of mistake in which you might come to an understanding with someone, but the respect is gone. And even if it's earned back, it's never the same. Sometimes in life, we cross the line of no return."

"Are you saying you think I've crossed the point of no return with my wife, Tom?" Dr. Peterson asked.

"I'm saying that life changes in the blink of an eye," Amore said. "To me, I just always look back at that one day – the day I decided to take a drink, which is, incidentally, when I hit it off with Lila. That's my life-altering mistake. Well, the first of a series of poor decisions... but a terrible error on my part, nonetheless. It was a real game-changer."

"But, technically, you found love that day," Dr. Peterson said. "I'm confused. You just said you identify that period of your life as a happy place – a time you can fall back on."

"I fall back because I feel like I can no longer push forward," Amore said.

Aug. 2, 1994
Status: Not delivered

*Dear Lila:*

*I'm sorry for the way things have gone. The man you once knew is gone, and I don't know when he'll be back. I am in the process of getting sober (trust me; it's a process) and hope that it brings me some level of peace.*

*Nevertheless, I am happy for you. Maybe one day our paths will cross again. If not, I will always look back fondly on the time we spent together.*

*Take care.*

*--Thomas*

# Twelve:
# The Separation

So," Dr. Peterson said, slowly sipping his third cup of coffee. "What are your plans from here?"

Long-term planning was a thing of the past for Amore. The question took him by surprise.

"I suppose I will probably head to a little place that I occasionally call home. If I don't go back to the shelter tonight – which I'm not particularly in a rush to do," Amore said, pointing to his battered face, "I will probably head toward the railroad tracks. I've got a little bunker of sorts that I patched together under the bridge... it stays mostly dry and free of wind."

"Why don't you come with me?" Dr. Peterson asked. "You can stay at my house as long as you like. I will make it my goal to help you out."

Amore's face – uncomfortable at best – told Dr. Peterson everything he needed to know.

"I mean, we'll work together to get you back on your feet. Wouldn't you at least like the chance to sleep in a warm bed? I have more than enough space. We can regroup in the morning. I know too many people not to help," Dr. Peterson pleaded.

"It's sure been nice chatting with you, Doc," Amore said. "I haven't had a two-way conversation like this in years. Nobody usually listens – or offers anything substantive in return."

"So then how about it, Tom?" Dr. Peterson asked.

"The thing is, Doc... it's over for me. This is the end of my road. This is who I am. I had potential, and I never fully realized it until it was too late. Once I let everyone down, I went on a continuous pattern of letting myself down time and time again. And now, I'll just wait to die. There is no comeback story for me, Doc. I am who I am; my scars will never fully heal. I only hope you can realize that what you have with your wife is not too far gone. You have a scratch on your surface; it won't scar unless you dig deeper."

"But, Tom," Dr. Peterson pleaded. "You are a well-spoken and seemingly intelligent, capable man. And quite philosophical, I must say. You have plenty to offer the world. Nothing is too far gone."

"I have my good days, and I have my bad days," Amore said.

"You can change, Tom," Dr. Peterson said. "You can change the world. Think about it: a homeless man who turns it all around. This story has legs."

"Not me, Doc," Amore said. "It's people like you who change the world. I'm a vagrant. It's probably best that I continue on the path I'm already on. I used to shake my finger at the government; I used to be a lover; but the people – they stopped listening. And eventually, the people who did listen either ran away or died. It's the cold, hard truth, Doc."

Aside from the subtle conversations taking place between the fellow snow-ins, Amore and Dr. Peterson sat in silence – occasionally making eye contact, but more often than not looking around the room.

Suddenly the sound of Dr. Peterson's phone ringing broke the awkward silence. It was his wife. As often was the case when the Petersons had minor squabbles, cooler heads prevailed.

"Honey, are you safe?" he asked her. "I'm stranded in a coffee shop along the train line."

The two spoke for a few minutes before Dr. Peterson made his final attempt at persuading Amore.

"Well, I guess that's it," he said to Amore. "I'm out of coffee and I suppose out of luck with trying to help you. My wife said the roads are lousy but drivable, so she is on her way to pick me up."

"If you decide you want to get back on track, here is my card," Dr. Peterson added, sliding his business card across the table. "I'm certain that I could help you find work and a place to live, if you are willing to commit the time and effort."

But then it happened – Amore had a change of heart.

"What type of work, Doc?" he asked. "What does the world want with a guy like me?"

"Well, I certainly can't promise this exact opportunity, but a good friend of mine owns an apartment complex, and he's looking for someone to assist the superintendent," Dr. Peterson said. "The pay would be all right, but more importantly, he'd probably put you up in an apartment for next to nothing – as long as you are handy and reliable, that is."

"I guess that would sure beat the shelter," Amore said. "And I suppose it would guarantee that my box of letters would stay dry."

"I'll tell you what," Dr. Peterson said. "I will reach out to my friend.

Let's meet here in two days at noon, and I will let you know what he says. Sound good?"

"Deal," Amore said. "Thank you, Doc. I don't know why you are taking interest in me, but thank you. I mean, quite honestly, I'm not certain that I want to change my life at this point. But again, maybe a dry place to keep my letters wouldn't be so bad. I just... this just seems too good – or too lucky – to be true."

Dr. Peterson smiled and let out a bit of laughter.

"You know, Tom," he said. "One of my mentors when I was growing up once told me something that has stuck with me for years: 'Always embrace luck. And the harder you work toward something, the luckier you will become.'"

Amore nodded as if thoroughly soaking in Dr. Peterson's words of wisdom.

"Embrace luck," he said.

## THIRTEEN:
## WIFE TO THE RESCUE

Irene Peterson parked her car – the wheel wells caked in a murky-colored, compact snow – in front of the coffee shop. She began dialing Preston's number, expecting him to be waiting inside the comfortable confines of the coffee house.

Before she transmitted the call, however, she squinted and noticed a man leaning against a nearby light pole. The man – slender, wearing an overcoat and a top hat – stood with his head down while the snow slammed him from all sides. He seemed unfazed. It couldn't be her husband, she thought.

And so, slightly curious, she pressed "Talk" on her phone, which had her husband's number already waiting in the balance.

Moments later, the yet-to-be-identified man reached for his pocket and pulled out a phone. Irene, who didn't even have the phone up to her head as she watched his actions, hung up and rolled down the passenger window.

"Preston!" she yelled. "Over here!"

He opened the passenger door, sliding his rear end in first while tapping his feet together to shake the snow loose from his boots.

"What on earth were you doing waiting outside?" Irene asked.

"It's been a long, long day, Irene," he said. "I never made it to my speaking engagement. I didn't pick up a book. And I didn't grade a paper or look at any data. But I'll be darned; I learned more today than I have in years."

"You have just been at this coffee shop all day, right?" Irene asked.

"Yes," he said. "And I think I finally have found what I've been searching for."

She rolled her eyes and let out a sigh.

"No, no," he said, laughing. "You are my rock, Irene. I knew that from the moment we met. But I had another one of those moments. You know how I'm always bemoaning that something is missing in my life – that my life's work is incomplete?"

"Yes, Preston," she said, a bit confounded by her complicated husband.

"Do you realize that I have won a Nobel Peace Prize, but I've never actually literally helped someone? I've never once stuck my hand out and said, 'Hey, can I help you?'" he said.

"Preston..." Irene said, equal parts irritated and amused. "I just... I just don't know, with you. How much coffee have you had, for heaven's sake?"

"About five gallons," he said quickly. "And before I say anything else, I just want to say how sorry I am for my behavior – not only this morning, but, well... for quite some time."

"It's okay, Preston," she said.

"No," he said, shaking his head. "I've spent so much of my life studying others and building up my own status that I have often neglected my own emotions – chiefly my love for you and how important it is to everything that I do."

Irene wasn't quite sure what to make of her husband's revelation.

"That's very sweet of you, Preston, but perhaps we need to get you home to rest," she said.

# FOURTEEN:
## THE ARRANGEMENT

John Coplan wasn't sure what he was getting into when Dr. Peterson invited him over for a Saturday afternoon lunch meeting at his house.

Coplan, a lifelong friend of Dr. Peterson's, was an urban planner and developer. He owned several properties throughout the city, including the one that Dr. Peterson hoped Amore would soon call home.

"To what do I owe the privilege of an invite to the Peterson abode?" Coplan asked as he walked through the front door.

Dr. Peterson laughed a bit.

"Right to business, huh?" he said with a smile. "You are going to kind of have to hear me out on this one, John. I have a rather unusual request. Let's take a seat, though. Irene put together a nice spread."

The longtime friends then did as most do when a bit of time has passed between meetings – they brought each other up to speed on their respective lives, though both are highly visible in the community.

"So, what is it that you wanted to discuss?" Coplan asked before taking a bite of his sandwich.

"Last time we talked, you were telling me how you needed to bring someone on board to help your superintendent," Dr. Peterson said. "I found someone who I think would be a nice fit."

A puzzled look came over Coplan's face.

"Although I'm happy to visit, you probably could have just given me a phone call about this," Coplan said. "We aren't talking about adding an executive."

"Well, there's a bit a catch," Dr. Peterson said. "He's currently homeless. I thought maybe you could bring him on board on a trial basis and let him rent one of the small, one-bedroom apartments."

"You want me to do *what*?" Coplan asked. "You can't be serious. I'm not in the charity business, Preston."

"I'm telling you," Dr. Peterson said. "Just give the guy a chance. What's the worst that can happen – you have to throw him out and find someone else? We have an opportunity to help relaunch a man's life here, John."

"Give me a break, Preston," Coplan said. "I don't have time for this crap. Is this really what you invited me here for? I need someone reliable, Preston – not a bum."

"There's just something about this guy, John," Dr. Peterson pleaded. "I'm telling you – he's got a heart of gold. He's sober, too, and has been for years, from what he was saying."

Coplan chuckled a bit, shaking his head in disbelief.

"How the hell did this even come about?" he asked. "You just go around talking to homeless people now?"

"It's a long story, but the gist of it is this: I met him on the train Monday afternoon," Dr. Peterson said. "We got to talking, so I asked if I could buy him a cup of coffee. Next thing you know, we were snowed in and one cup of coffee turned into three over the course of nearly eight hours. I wouldn't ask for this if I didn't feel so strongly about it, John; you know me better than that. And when do I ask for favors from you?

"Some people just need a second chance," Dr. Peterson continued. "Most people never get it, but I'm telling you – this guy might just make something of it, if we help him. He's not your typical drifter. He speaks eloquently, and above all else, like I said, he's sober."

Coplan, holding both hands in the air as if he was surrendering, took a deep breath in, and let out a lengthy exhale.

"Okay, Preston," he said. "I will entertain the idea. Bring him by the office Monday."

## FIFTEEN:
## RETURNING FROM HELL

Amore thought long and hard about Dr. Peterson's offer as he paced the windswept streets of Buffalo with a lifetime of thoughts marching through his head.

His encounter with Dr. Peterson had him thinking more clearly than he had in quite some time. And for Amore, who had more time on his hands than the average man, that wasn't necessarily a good thing.

He replayed in his head the moments that led him to homelessness – chiefly, his experience in the Vietnam War and the years that followed – and pondered if he deserved yet another chance.

When Amore returned from Vietnam, it was not to fanfare. The only people waiting at the airport were seemingly those who screamed profanity. There were others who spat on him.

Amore landed on October 24, 1972, at Fort Lewis, Washington, where he was given a uniform to change into before being discharged.

Surfing through an angry airport crowd, he made his way to the first available bathroom to shed his uniform. He just wanted a sense of normalcy back in his life. He was never the guy whom people hated.

Yet, when he returned home, people called him a murderer. It was a tough pill to swallow, and the sad part for Amore was: they were right.

Less than a month into his service, while on observation post, Amore saw a member of the Viet Cong heading in his direction.

It was a familiar look, as it was once again an enemy in an opposing Army's uniform. But this enemy wasn't just trying to take him to the ground momentarily; this enemy was trying to put him six feet under the ground – for eternity.

So he shot and killed the would-be rebel.

That moment always remained in the back of Amore's mind somewhere, but it certainly wasn't a memory that he shared with others.

Although he was a tough-as-nails athlete, he was also a bit of a gentle giant. His efforts in the Vietnam War weren't courageous, he thought. In his eyes, he'd murdered another human being, and that's all that mattered. Everything he ever envisioned about being a soldier – namely, becoming a true American hero – was erased in that moment.

Amore spent nearly three years in Vietnam and probably slept for what the average person gets in a half year. And when he got home, that only got worse. The only thing that put his nightmares at ease was alcohol, because he would drink himself into a blacked-out haze.

Lila Stevenson came back around, but it wasn't the same. What's more, Amore wasn't the same. Sometimes they'd try to pretend like everything was okay, but it was hardly a romance novel in the making. At times, they sat there enjoying a cup of coffee, and every now and then Amore couldn't hold back a tear or two. She would constantly ask him what was wrong, but there was no easy answer.

And as day turned to night, coffee turned to booze and Amore turned into a babbling, drunken buffoon. Most of the time, Stevenson avoided going to the tavern with him... as she should have. But soon, she started avoiding him for much – if not all – of the next day, too.

Amore often pointed to singular moments in his life that he called "game-changers." The first day he drank was certainly a step in the wrong direction, but there were many more to follow.

Wavering on what to do with the latest game-changer – this time, potentially for the better – Amore thought back on a conversation with Stevenson.

"Thomas," she said one day, not long after he returned from Vietnam. "It's 3 p.m., and you absolutely stink of alcohol. Is that from last night? And how is that even possible?"

She was disgusted.

"I guess so," he recalled admitted. "Who cares?"

The words "who cares" would bounce between Amore's ears for years to come. Who cares? Who cares? God. *What a stupid thing to say,* Amore later thought – amid his sober years.

She walked out the door that day without another word. Amore took a stroll down to the tavern about an hour later, still not fully recovered from the night before.

"Lila bolted on me," he told the bartender, who was the only other person in the room.

"I got something that will cheer you up," the bartender said, peering in either direction to make sure they were alone. "You ever tried cocaine?"

"I'm not really sure," Amore said. "I sniffed something funky during the war, but I don't know if it was cocaine. But whatever, man. Will it cure my hangover?"

And cure his hangover it did. But it also firmly planted Amore's feet among the world's lost souls — the barroom dwellers who jibber jabber until the sun comes up.

The once-prized college football recruit-turned-soldier hit a brick wall. And at the time, he hardly realized how beautiful a life he was missing on the other side.

But in 2014, as he looked backward, he was certainly aware of the life that he lost out on back then. Increasingly, he felt shame and unworthy of another chance.

# Sixteen:
# Judgment Day

Prior to his chance encounter with Amore, Dr. Peterson lived a meaningful life, but he became a bit complacent, like a musician near the end of his career, playing the same old song for more than 40 years. He worked tirelessly but was becoming increasingly confrontational with his wife and was struggling to reinvent himself.

Through Amore, he saw hope; he saw the possibility of new life through a man living so close to the edge. Dr. Peterson spent the majority of his adult life assigning meaning to research by making sense of data, but in Amore, it was just a matter of timing. Dr. Peterson thought if he just would have had this opportunity earlier, things would have been all right for him a long time ago.

And so, the big day came. Dr. Peterson arrived at Coplan's office at 7:30 a.m. on Monday. Amore was scheduled to arrive at 8.

"Well, is your guy going to show?" Coplan asked.

"I spoke with him yesterday," Dr. Peterson said. "He has everything to gain and nothing to lose, so I can't imagine why he would bail on me now. He seemed quite enthusiastic about rejoining the workforce."

"We'll see," Coplan said, still unsure of Dr. Peterson's plan.

"John, I spent eight hours with this guy," Dr. Peterson said. "I heard in graphic detail – blow by blow – his life story… the good and the bad. And he certainly has some redeeming qualities. You won't believe how well-spoken he is. The funny thing is, he's even up on his current events. The guy reads the paper cover-to-cover, daily. He knew exactly who I was and is well aware of your development efforts."

"Okay," Coplan said. "Care for a cup of coffee?"

Dr. Peterson, sporting a noticeable look of disappointment at Coplan's lack of interest, nodded in agreement.

"Yeah. I suppose," he said. "Thank you."

And so Dr. Peterson once again found himself in an obstinate stare-down while sipping on a cup of coffee. But this time, the man across the table – in this case, a busy but organized desk – was far from a bloodied vagabond.

Coplan was resplendent in his tailor-fit, three-piece suit. His salt-and-pepper hair was neatly combed, with a perfect part. He had a Wall Street look, with matching bravado. His confidence was enough to fill the room and intimidate anyone who walked through the door.

Time passed. "Are we done here?" Coplan asked, looking at his watch. "It's nearly 8:30. I've got little time to waste as it is, and I've already wasted 30 minutes."

"I suppose we are, John," Dr. Peterson said, setting his mug atop Coplan's desk. "I'm sorry I wasted your time."

The two shook hands, but Coplan was quick to refocus his attention on the day ahead. Without so much as a goodbye, Coplan picked up the phone from his desk and forged ahead.

Dr. Peterson wasn't willing to give up that quickly.

He paced up and down the sidewalk outside of Coplan's office for an hour. The Monday morning business crowd – light by a city's standards – wasn't enough to lose sight of a person. But it didn't matter if Dr. Peterson was in midtown Manhattan – his eyes were dialated like a sniper's, and Amore was his target.

Suddenly, however, a voice came from behind him.

"'Scuse me, sir," the man's voice said. "Can you spare some change?"

Dr. Peterson's heart raced, hoping he'd turn to see Amore.

"Oh," he said, disappointed. "I thought you might be someone I am looking for."

The man squirmed a bit.

"You a cop?" he asked.

"No," Dr. Peterson said. "I'm looking for my friend, Tom Amore. Do you know him?"

"'Scuse me, sir," the man said again. "Can you spare some change?"

Like a long-dormant volcano, Dr. Peterson erupted unexpectedly – the first in a series of meltdowns for a man who had spent so much of his life in a state of level-headedness.

"Come on!" he screamed. "I asked you a question! That's your answer – another question? The same one that you just asked me?"

More confused than usual, the panhandler meandered into a nearby alley. Dr. Peterson stood alone and in distress, spouting off, his words dissipating into the cool winter air.

"This was supposed to work!" he screamed, with his head tilted back and arms raised towards the sky. "Does nobody believe in a good comeback story?"

## Seventeen:
## The Lone Wolf

It had been three months since Amore saw Dr. Peterson. And despite knowing it was coming well in advance of his chance meeting with Dr. Peterson, Amore's time at the homeless shelter had come to an end.

With the shelter door closing, Amore thought at length about Dr. Peterson's offer. It wasn't so much that he regretted not accepting the chance at a new life, but that his mind spun uncontrollably with shame for letting down the one person who'd showed him any sign of concern.

He sat on a perch in front of an abandoned building – one of his many go-to spots to pass the time – but this was no ordinary day in the life of a homeless man. There was no ulterior motive for his public loitering; he had hardly a second to invest in thinking about panhandling.

Amore sat with his head in his hands, his fingers woven through the straggly horseshoe remainder of his hair. A single tear fell from his eye, plummeting to the step upon which his feet were resting. Not but a moment later, his eyes opened up like Niagara Falls.

It had been years since Amore felt such emotion; frankly, he had been going day-to-day for so long that he never really stopped to think about how much time had passed. His conversation with Dr. Peterson had made him realize how bleak things had become. His life was only a thing of the past – a story of lost love in a rickety box – and was nothing like it used to be: full of hope for the future.

After drying the last of his tears, Amore pulled himself up from the perch. He looked at his reflection in a window. What he saw staring back was startling.

The unfamiliar man glaring back from the abandoned building was devoid of Amore's once Huck-Finn-handsome teenage looks and a red-hot future. It hit Amore in the mouth like a right hook from a prizefighter.

His free-flowing blonde hair had turned to a chalky gray; his glossy teeth were now rotted (those still dangling from his gums, that is); and his skin had gone from silky smooth to as dry as a sundrenched baseball mitt.

Although the calendar continued moving forward, Amore spent years in one place, rotting away like a plant deprived of water.

The discovery of his faded looks, however, was enough to force him to make a drastic change. He realized that life wasn't going to get much better unless he traveled along a different road than the four-block radius he ordinarily traipsed.

With a frayed backpack over his shoulder and his wooden box under his arm, Amore set out on a journey. But rather than heading into the heart of downtown, he maneuvered south of the city. He had no true plan to follow, other than to do the opposite of what he had become accustomed to.

Amore walked for three miles, abandoned buildings, bulldozed lots, and blight in his path, before he settled on setting up camp in the city's three-square-mile nature preserve. Although he had technically been living a survivalist lifestyle, he figured it was time to put some of his long-since-discarded military survival tactics to practice. Living in seclusion, he thought, would be best for everyone.

As he surveyed the land, he was immediately struck with a bit of dumb luck: an assumed child-constructed fort. With three full walls, a roof and a somewhat stable floor – it would certainly do the trick, he thought.

With the sun still shining brightly overhead, Amore unloaded his backpack, including a tarp, a sleeping bag, a lighter, and a Swiss army knife. Shortly thereafter, he gathered a bundle of loose debris from the forest to create a fire – twigs for kindling and larger broken branches for logs.

Within an hour of finding the fort, he suddenly had more to speak of than he had in nearly a decade. His confidence began to rise.

But there was still one enormous obstacle Amore had to overcome: Where was his next meal going to come from?

Knowing that the nature preserve had a range of animals that included wild turkey and deer, Amore once again recalled his military training and began slowly creeping through the forest, stalking his prey.

The sun began to retire over the nearby lake, and Amore knew it was game time. A herd of deer began grazing in the field. Others drank from the lake. Amore, who hadn't spoken a word in two days – not even to himself – began to chuckle. He knew the deer would be repeat customers; even if he didn't capture one that night, he would have plenty of opportunities in the days and nights to follow.

He quickly shuffled back to his camp, bouncing lightly on his toes to avoid creating a stir. Once situated, he chiseled one of the longer, thicker branches into a spear – the first weapon that came to mind in an attempt to take down a deer.

Beaming with newfound enthusiasm, the ex-soldier once again was faced with a mission.

He returned to the lake an hour later, freshly crafted harpoon in hand. To his surprise, there were still several deer feeding on the grass.

Of course, he also realized that taking down the large animal would be no easy task. He wasn't half the man he used to be, so throwing the spear wasn't an option. The only way, he thought, was to sneak up on one and stab it with precision.

He failed miserably.

And so Amore was left once more with nothing more than a collection of his thoughts. But at least there was a process – a plan of sorts, he thought.

## Eighteen:
## Honey, We Need To Talk

A few days had passed, and it was business as usual for Dr. Peterson: work, work and more work. But one thing was decidedly different: His compassion for his wife had come out of its longstanding hibernation.

It was almost as if seeing something so close to death made him realize how precious time really is.

"Irene," he said softly as she was preparing dinner. "I think maybe we should take a vacation – just the two of us. What do you say?"

"Vacation" was hardly the native tongue in the Peterson household.

"Is it April Fools' Day, or is this how you are breaking the news to me that you are having an affair?" she asked with laughter in her voice.

"No. I am serious," he said candidly. "I've spent too much of my life working – or thinking about work when I'm not at work – and frankly, I think it's time we enjoy the life we've built together."

Cautiously optimistic, she smirked before responding.

"All right, Preston," she said. "But I'm warning you – no email, and no answering your phone. And why this sudden change, might I ask?"

"It goes back to what I told you that night you picked me up from the coffee shop," he said. "I cannot stop thinking about that homeless man, Tom. I can't stop pondering what his life could have been – who he could have been. And then I wonder... does it really even matter? What's this whole thing about? What's the difference between Tom and me? Is this life just about collecting more material objects? Are Tom's day-to-day struggles a product of his upbringing?"

"Preston," she interrupted, stirring a pot of semi-frozen sauce on the stove. "Why are you so worked up over this man? You have become the man you are through tireless work – work that has greatly benefited society as a whole."

"I suppose you're right," he said. "I'll try not to think about it. The only thing on my mind for the rest of the night is that delicious-smelling sauce you've got going over there, and planning our vacation, my love."

"Well, that's fine," she said. "But I have to admit that after dinner, I made plans for us to go out for a couple drinks with Steve and Mary. Can we put the planning on hold until tomorrow? Or maybe discuss it tonight over drinks?"

The Petersons weren't much for hitting the town, but they occasionally wined and dined with Steve and Mary McGee, a fellow well-to-do couple that lived next door.

"Yeah; that sounds nice," he said. "We haven't been out in ages. It'll be nice to let our hair down for once."

Irene could barely hold in her laughter.

"Oh, please, Preston," she said with a chuckle. "You're going to let *your* hair down?"

"You're absolutely right," he said. "In fact, I'm going to pour myself a

Scotch as we speak. Care for a glass of wine while you cook?"

She obliged, and before long Preston, who began acting even more outside of his element, offered up a toast.

"Here's to new beginnings," he said. "Cheers!"

"New beginnings?" his puzzled wife asked. "You're acting awfully strange, my dear. Although, I must admit – I don't hate it. But something seems a bit out of character."

"I think that enough is enough," Preston said. "I think I'm going to retire. We have more money than we can reasonably spend in this lifetime; the kids are self-sufficient; and everything we own is paid for. What's the point? We need to live before it's no longer an option."

Irene looked as overcome with joy as an unsuspecting woman who has just received a proposal.

"Are you serious?" she asked, a radiant glow on her face. "Preston, it's just... well, I totally agree. But are you sure?"

He swirled his neatly poured Scotch, nodded his head, and shrugged his shoulders as if there wasn't much else to think about.

"That's it," he said. "I've been thinking a lot about life lately, which I'm sure you've picked up on. And it's, without question, time that I turn the page. It's time for you and I to start a new chapter – one without stress, in which we focus on enjoying one another again... like when we first met. Well, I suppose I should backtrack a bit – in that next chapter, I will focus on making up for lost time – time that I spent selfishly working on my career."

And with that, the doorbell sounded.

"I'll get it, honey!" he said with a ring to his voice.

Preston ran to the door like a kid expecting his friends for a game of backyard baseball.

"Steve, Mary!" he said. "Come on in! I have some exciting news!"

Preston let his guests in and quickly returned to the kitchen, where he fetched four tumbler glasses. He poured Scotch for himself and Steve and filled the ladies' glasses with something a bit sweeter.

"Before we go anywhere, I have a bit of an announcement," he said, sliding the glasses around the glossy-topped center island in their kitchen. "I decided today that I am retiring."

The room quickly filled with joy, and before everyone knew it, one celebratory shot turned into two – fast-tracking an unexpected night of gloves-off drunkenness for everyone. Especially the ordinarily one-and-done drinker, Preston Peterson.

"The heck with it!" he said, raising his empty glass in the air. "I'm drinkin' tonight! No, no – *we're* drinkin' tonight!"

There wasn't a drop of objection, so the next logical step was saun-tering to the nearby watering hole. When they arrived, the wives made a trip to the bathroom together, which allowed time for Preston to buy a quick round of shots.

"Ohh, okaaayyyyy," Steve said, looking toward the bathroom. "Quickly, though. And no word of this to the ladies!"

When their wives returned, Steve and Preston were in deep conver-sation, which led to the couples splitting off into opposite-gender pairs for quite some time.

"So what made you do it?" Steve asked his friend. "I mean, I thought you would be a guy who worked until time ran out."

"I thought so, too, Steve," Preston said, holding up a finger as if about to spew a profound thought. "But you know something? I'll tell you something. I met this strange guy – a bum."

Steve erupted in laughter.

"So what you are saying is: you met a man?" he asked, laughing even harder.

"Lemme finish," Preston said, also drunkenly cackling. "It's not like that. It's just – I don't know. I can't stop thinking about this guy. He just... well, he changed my entire outlook on life. I've always questioned every-thing; you know that. But now I'm questioning the things I never thought I would: areas of my life that I thought I had buttoned up. This guy's even got me questioning if everything I've ever done professionally even means anything. Was it all a complete waste?"

Steve looked perplexed.

"It's okay to question the meaning of life every now and then, Pres-ton," he said. "And I am glad that you are retiring. But don't for a second discount your career; you have made a world's difference. Take a walk down the hallway in your house for a reminder. Take a look at that pile of books that you've published. Heck, ask one of your former students."

"I dunno," Preston said, shrugging. "But whatever... I'm retiring. It's time for me to live a little."

"Are you a happy man?" Steve asked. "You seemed happy when I got here tonight – more happy than I've seen you in years, in fact."

Preston, who had one eye closed, peered to the bottom of his empty beer glass with the other and thought about his words for a minute.

"Yeah," he said. "I'm pretty sure that I'm happy. Or maybe I'm... I'm just... maybe I'm just totally drunk."

About a minute passed, and then both men erupted in drunken laughter.

"Yeah," Preston said. "I'm totally blasted. But I'm gonna... I'm gonna find that friggin' guy, Steve; I absolutely have to. But... ya know... don't tell my wife."

# Nineteen:
# And The Days Go By

Days turned into months after Dr. Peterson promised his wife a vacation and less emphasis on work, yet life at the Peterson residence remained quite similar to the 40 preceding years.

The routine: breakfast, read the Wall Street Journal, go to work, return, and continue research until it was time to call it a night.

However, there was one noticeable change that became woven into the fabric of the daily regimen: Preston's obsession with finding Amore.

He continuously found a way to bring up Amore's name – and frankly, it drove his wife up the wall. What's more, it quite literally kept him up at night.

"Honey – would you look at this?" he said to his wife one morning, reading the Wall Street Journal over breakfast. "The minimum wage is climbing toward $10 per hour, and fast-food workers are seeking $15."

"That's crazy," she said. "Who would have thought?"

He should have quit while he was ahead.

"Tom could be making $10 to $15 per hour!" he insisted. "Why wouldn't he have just met me at Coplan's that day?"

Irene was about to take a bite of an omelet, but the sound of Amore's name forced her to drop her fork, which clanked off her plate and scattered bits of egg across the kitchen table.

"Preston!" she said, frustration obvious in her tone and expression. "Enough with that creepy guy! He is not making any money because he is not working for it! How many times do I have to explain this to you?"

"I know," he said, cowering a bit. "I'm sorry. I just really want to help him. It's consuming me."

"You are a brilliant man, Preston," she said, calming her voice a bit. "But I cannot stand to see you like this. Enough is enough. Maybe you should talk to someone."

Although her advice was quite practical, Irene, too, should have quit while she was ahead.

"That's an insult to my intelligence!" Preston said. "I am perfectly sane! I'm sorry that I want to help someone. God forbid we fight for humanity!"

Irene rolled her eyes and the couple continued eating in silence.

*So much for that vacation*, she thought.

## Twenty:
## The Unceremonious Retirement

**D**r. Peterson's retirement announcement came as a shock. He had been a staple at the University at Buffalo and in professional circles for decades. His impact on the field had far exceeded any of his colleagues' – and for that, the university was forever in debt to him.

But as he neared the end of the road, he grew increasingly strange.

Perhaps it was the knowledge of his fate – knowing a definitive date in which everything he worked for would come to an end; it was a death, of sorts. Or perhaps it was his obsession with Amore and, more specifically, why he'd rejected assistance. Maybe it was a combination of both.

In either case, one thing was for sure: Dr. Peterson's wheels could not stop spinning when it came to Amore. And it began to show.

Late in the spring semester – Dr. Peterson's grand finale –word of his changing persona hit the mainstream. Dr. Peterson had assigned his students one of his books to read: a step-by-step guide to the human life cycle.

"Well," he said to the class, standing on the ground floor of a crowded lecture hall. "What does this all mean?"

The question seemed loaded. And so the lecture hall remained at a collective standstill.

"Anyone?" he asked.

Finally, a student sitting in the middle of the lecture hall (perhaps 15 rows deep) perked up.

"Are you asking us, 'What is the meaning of life?'" she called out.

Dr. Peterson scratched his chin and paced back and forth before responding.

"You want to know the meaning of life?" he asked. "It's all a bunch of nonsense!"

"This," he said, swirling his hands frantically, pointing up and around. "This is all a biiiiiiiig show, and we are the main characters! What does it all mean? I don't even know anymore."

Thoughts of his inability to help Amore raced through his mind. He had been playing it cool at home and with his peers, doing his best to not talk about it; but all the while, it was consuming him.

And then the lid came off.

"We are all just puppets! You want to see life? Here it is!" he screamed, just seconds before winding up like a baseball pitcher and throwing his porcelain coffee mug at the brick wall behind him. "That is life! A big, shattered mess!"

The classroom once again turned silent.

"Or how about this? This is life!" he again exclaimed, flipping a near-by desk.

"I've spent my entire life analyzing every little detail of life – both scientific and philosophic – and I've just recently realized one thing: It all means nothing if you don't actually live a day in your life. I spent my entire life working, studying, and then studying what I studied. And for what?" Dr. Peterson ranted.

"Dr. Peterson," another student interrupted. "If I may – your body of work was all worth it. We have all learned so much from you – lessons that I know for certain that I will look back upon."

Dr. Peterson let loose a mocking laugh before addressing the student's comment.

"No need to placate me," he said. "That's a crock, and you know it. I've worked and worked, and now I'm closer to death than I've ever been, and I'm realizing what I've missed. I've never even watered my own garden! We pay someone to do it! You know why? Because I'm rich and I'm apparently too busy. I can't even recall a time that I did my own laundry. Am I even a grown man? But at least I have a handful of awards on my wall, and you all allegedly respect me, right? What a life, I tell ya."

After his nuclear meltdown of sorts, Dr. Peterson glanced over the wreckage and scanned the room full of stunned, silent students. Without further explanation, he closed his eyes and shook his head a bit before making his way to the door.

Word of his eruption spread like a wildfire in the wind.

As Dr. Peterson opened the door to his Mercedes, his cell phone rang. It was Dr. Frank Belemi, the school's president.

A lengthy conversation took place, with Dr. Peterson doing very little talking.

"I understand," he said often.

"Duly noted," he added.

"I will be all right," he pleaded. "No need to worry about me. Thank you for your concern."

And with that, Dr. Peterson's career came to an abrupt end – an unceremonious completion to an otherwise-celebrated journey. No balloons. No parade. Not even a slice of sugary cake. There was no sweet ending for Dr. Preston Peterson.

He drove off the university grounds for the last time and into the gray, gloomy spring afternoon. The air not yet turned warm, and murky, sloppy snow was still piled along the sides of the road. It was the most unusual of scenarios for Dr. Peterson, who seldom took a day off, to be driving home in the middle of a workday.

## Twenty-One:
## Under the Sun

When Amore set out into the wilderness, for the first time in a long time, he was daring to be different. And for the first time as a homeless man, he was going to attempt to live completely independently with no handouts or shelters.

It took trial and error, with emphasis on the error, but eventually his survival skills resurfaced.

After the laughable attempt at hunting deer with a hand-carved spear, Amore turned his focus on capturing a wild turkey... or any small game animal that he could capture with his limited resources.

He sat on the stump outside of his new compound and thought long and hard about his time at West Point. For a moment, he fell into a bit of a daydream, recalling the roar of the crowd when he piled up 193 yards and two touchdowns to help the Army beat its rival, the Navy.

Reflecting on the good times – especially his football career, which he hadn't thought about in some time – put a smile on his face. It also helped him recall another important moment from his time at West Point: a survival course that he and the fellow plebes were required to take during freshman year.

"A twitch-up snare!" Amore proclaimed. "That's what I need!"

To make the twitch-up snare, he needed to find two forked sticks, each with a long and a short leg. Then he bent the twitch-up and marked the trail below it. He drove the long leg of one forked stick firmly into the ground.

*What's the next step?* he thought.

"Think, Tom... think," he said out loud to himself. "Oh yeah!"

"Ensure the cut on the short leg of this stick is parallel to the ground," he said, following his own instructions as he went. "Tie the long leg of the remaining forked stick to a piece of cordage secured to the twitch-up. Cut the short leg so that it catches on the short leg of the other forked stick."

He then extended a noose over the trail and set the trap by bending the twitch-up and engaging the short legs of the forked sticks.

Now he just had to hope that an animal would catch its head in the noose to pull the forked sticks apart, allowing the twitch-up to spring up and hang the prey.

But rather than sit idle, Amore decided to set a few twitch-up traps around the perimeter of his living quarters.

As he was setting up his fourth such trap, he heard a snap followed by what sounded like the crack of a whip.

"No flippin' way," he said to himself, standing up slowly as he set the fourth and final trap. "Please, God. Tell me this already worked."

He ran toward the sound, bushwhacking the landscape with his hands along the way.

When he got to the trap – the first that he had set – he couldn't believe his eyes. A rabbit, twitching feverishly amid its final few living moments, hung from the tree.

He dropped to his knees and erupted in laughter.

"Wooooooooooo!" he screamed. "That's what I'm talking about! I'm back, baby!"

Indeed, Thomas Amore once again felt like Thomas Amore. The young boy who'd once beamed with confidence had reemerged in the form of a 67-year-old man.

## Twenty-Two:
## Welcome Home, Pal

It was tough to say who was more caught off guard: Irene at the sight of her husband arriving home from work in the middle of the day, or Preston at the tone of his wife's demand.

"What are you doing home so early?" she asked as he opened the front door.

"It's a long story, but right now I think I may just take a nap," he said. "I'm not feeling all that well."

"Preston," she said. "There's something I want to talk to you about, first."

"Can it wait until later, sweetie?" he asked. "I'm awfully tired."

"It cannot," she said, letting out a sigh.

"Very well," he said, setting down his brief case before kicking off his shoes and hanging his coat in the inside closet.

Irene asked her husband to join her in the family room, where she had prepared a light snack. The two sat down comfortably, but there was nothing comfortable about the mood of the room in the moments that followed.

"Well," he said. "What's on your mind?"

"Preston," she said. "I think... well... I think we should talk about the possibility of either a separation or divorce."

Preston's face was blank – completely emotionless. He sat completely still and stared straight ahead, not looking at his wife and not at anything in particular. He had absolutely nothing to say - or at least, couldn't get the words out.

The two sat in complete silence for more than two minutes before Irene chimed in.

"Preston," she said. "Do you have anything to say?"

He remained silent and slowly shook his head from side to side.

"There is no love here, Preston!" she insisted. "And there hasn't been in years! I know you are smart enough to understand! I can't even re-member the last time we felt any bit of love for one another."

He still had no words.

"Please, Preston!" she said. "Say something – anything!"

Again slowly shaking his head from side to side, he dug deep for a response.

"What is there to say?" he asked. "Today I've been told by two of my most trusted allies – my wife and my employer of more than 40 years – that I'm no longer welcome. I thought I had a full chapter of my life to look forward to. I had this dream recently. It was just you and I, and we did all the things that most couples do – like working around the house together. I want to mow the lawn and water the garden. And I want to do those things with you."

"It's too late for all that," she said. "It's too late for that."

He stared blankly.

"I don't know what's happening to you, Preston," she said. "But it seems to me that you are the only one who's not realizing that things are changing – you're changing. Did you get fired?"

"Well, not fired," he said. "But I will not be finishing out the year as I had arranged."

"Like it even matters," she responded. "We've got more money than we can ever spend, anyway. You didn't even need to work anymore, but you chose to only to pad your own enormous ego."

"*We*? We have more money than we can spend? *We*?" he asked, with an angry smirk growing across his face. "*I* have more money! *I* earned every penny that this house has ever seen!"

"Well," she said. "We'll see what the lawyer has to say, Preston. If my memory serves me correctly, I never signed a prenuptial agreement."

"You foolish bitch!" he screamed, with a sequence of additional expletives that followed. "You've got to be kidding me!"

He stormed off toward the garage.

"I didn't mean that, Preston!" she called, frantically backtracking on her previous statement. "It's not even about the money! I don't want your money!"

He stopped for a moment and shook his head before continuing toward the garage.

"Where are you going? We're not done talking," she said.

"I bought some grass seed on the way home," he said. "I will be outside. There's a spot in the back yard that needs attention."

"*What*?" she asked with a decidedly confused ring to her voice.

"First of all, it's only 36 degrees outside. That seed will most certainly die. And that's your response to losing your job and wife – planting grass seed?"

"If it dies, it dies," he said. "It might as well – everything else I touch seems to die, so what's a $13 bag of grass seed? File your divorce papers, and do whatever it is you have to do. Just leave me alone."

And so Preston – never much of a do-it-yourselfer at home – took to the back yard, angrily spiking handfuls of grass seed. His wife watched from inside, standing with her hands on her hips.

"Preston!" she yelled, after opening the back door to the house. "Won't you please come in here? We need to talk. For the love of God."

Preston, who had his back to the house, turned around. But the look on his face – his grinding teeth and fire-engine red cheeks – said enough. She shut the door.

## Twenty-Three:
## Changing With the Times

It was October, and life had become rather simple for Dr. Peterson in only seven months.

Gone were the days of shaping the minds of others or spending the wee hours of the night hammering away on the keyboard of his home-office computer to churn out another bestseller.

He and his wife didn't go through with a divorce, but Dr. Peterson packed his bags and willingly offered his longtime mate the house.

Dr. Peterson – a doctor only on paper, these days – seemed to have gone through a full-blown metamorphosis.

He read more than he wrote and listened more than he spoke. His ordinarily flawlessly shaven face was hidden behind a heavy salt-and-pepper beard. Throughout his professional career, Dr. Peterson kept his hair short and parted to the right; but in the wake of his separation and freefall from professional circles, he let it grow longer. And the most noticeable change of all became visible in his eyes, which conveyed an unspoken pain.

Lonely and quietly seeking answers of a new variety, Dr. Peterson took to his new independent Saturday morning routine: He walked from his quaint two-bedroom apartment to Second Sip Café, where he would have breakfast and read the newspaper before taking a stroll to the nearby outdoor farmer's market.

For a man who became a known figure throughout his career, Dr. Peterson had become an unknown – just another face in the crowd.

But one day, things moved a little out of the new ordinary. Following his breakfast, Dr. Peterson was sifting through a table of locally grown lettuce when he caught something out of the corner of his eye and quickly snapped his head in its direction. He set down the head of lettuce and began squinting, as if adjusting his eyes like binoculars.

*No – it couldn't be, he thought. Is that… Amore?*

"That son of a pup," he proclaimed, much to the surprise of the man standing behind the produce table.

Hardly a second later, Dr. Peterson took off running, weaving between people and bumping into others.

"Excuse me, pardon me, coming through," he said frantically. "Sorry, excuse me, sorry."

With his eyes half shut, Amore – with his box secured to his side under his arm – walked slowly down the congested city sidewalk. Despite the fact that the autumn air temperature hovered at about 50 degrees, sweat ran down the back of his once-white T-shirt while the top of his head boiled to a volcanic red.

"Hey!" Dr. Peterson yelled as he approached Amore. "Tom! Tom!"

Amore halted his snail-like pace and turned to face his pursuer.

Before Amore could even think of getting a word out, Dr. Peterson let him have it.

"I had the world ready to be handed over on a silver platter for you, Tom!" he yelled, loud enough for passersby to hear. "I was ready to take you under my wing and you just completely left me high and dry! You made a complete fool of me! You're too smart and have too good of a heart to be out here like this! Look at you; you look freakin' terrible! This all could have changed. I mean, Jesus H. Christ... what did I tell you about luck?"

Amore nodded with what little energy he had.

"She left you, didn't she, Preston?" Amore asked softly.

Dr. Peterson shook his head in disbelief.

"Yeah, but..." he said. "What the hell? That has nothing to do with any of this."

"This was never about me, Preston," Amore said, coughing between his thoughts.

Suddenly, Amore began to gasp for air, perspiring at an abnormal rate. His cough turned into more of a pant, and without warning, he dropped to his knees and fell limply onto his side.

"Somebody help!" Dr. Peterson yelled as he dropped to his knees to check for a pulse. "Call 911!"

Thomas Amore was without a pulse. Dr. Peterson relentlessly performed CPR until the paramedics arrived, at which point they ushered him to the side.

Amore's treasured box crumbled underneath the weight of his body, sending its contents in all directions.

Dr. Peterson, still within a stone's throw of Amore, grabbed the first letter he could get his hands on. He unfolded one of its two creases and glanced at the first paragraph.

"You said we would grow old together, Thomas," the letter read. "You promised to never leave my side. I wanted that, too, my love. Please be well – and please find it in your heart to forgive me. I hope with more time you will understand that I never meant to hurt you."

A tear slid down Dr. Peterson's cheek as he closed his eyes and quivered. He could read no further. Rather than trying to play God with Amore's life any more than he already had, he gave the writer her wish and carefully placed the letter in Amore's pocket while the man was being moved into the back of an ambulance.

"Hey!" one of the paramedics yelled. "You'll have to back off, sir!"

Dr. Peterson apologized emphatically and quickly stepped aside.

"Can you at least tell me where you're taking him?" he asked.

"Sister's Hospital," a paramedic yelled back.

As Amore was taken off by ambulance, Dr. Peterson picked up the broken pieces of Amore's box, grabbing as many of the letters as he could find along the way.

## Twenty-Four:
## It Was All a Dream. Or Was It?

He was alone.

Given his recent renewed sense of optimism, he might have predicted things would work out differently. Someone who had received such a gift would never simply continue life as it had been before. But if the past was any indication, he should have known.

And here it was again: the holiday time of year – the loneliest time of the year for those without a family or home. The calendar served as a reminder that a new year was approaching – a time when many people set goals and aim to change for the better.

The change went much deeper than a season or a few new white hairs in his beard. It went under his skin – as deep as his soul, if he permitted himself to subscribe to such a notion.

*Life was like that*, he thought. It could strip everything away from you in the blink of an eye. It certainly had before; so this was no different.

But unlike the past, he came to realize it could restore everything you had lost – or give you even more, in fact, than you'd ever had – with the same lightning-bolt speed.

He knew that now, he quickly came to realize.

But this was no ordinary day, even by Amore's standards. As his vision caught up to his thought process, his surroundings became increasingly alarming. His eyes scanned the room – his body was belly-up and motionless – from left to right. He opened his mouth to call for help, but his throat was coarse beyond the ability of words, his tongue glued firmly in its place.

He sat up at once, only to be flattened by a pain that dashed up his side and forced a chirp from his vocal chords, which had been held speechless just moments before.

His body trembled while his eyes – now fully open – raced in terror. A feeding tube prevented him from speaking clearly, and so he let out a painful shriek.

"Mr. Amore, please calm down," a women's voice called to him from afar, backed by the sound of shoes tip-tapping closer. "Everything is okay. Everything is okay."

The woman, a nurse in the hospital that he had been admitted to a couple months prior, slowly removed the feeding tube and offered Amore a glass of water. With his hands shaking uncontrollably, he gulped down as much as he could.

"M-m-more," he begged.

"What happened, and where am I?" he asked, with panic in voice and a tear dripping slowly down his cheek. "What day is it?"

"Well, first I must tell you: it's Christmas Eve," she said, pointing out the window. The ground, blanketed in snow, glistened in the rare December sunshine. "You must be a religious man, Mr. Amore. It is a true miracle that you survived."

His face went blank and again he struggled for words.

"You were in a coma," the nurse advised him. "Your body had an extreme reaction to the high level of PCBs, mirex, chlordane and DDT that we found in your blood – likely a reaction to eating an infected animal."

"But, what?" he interrupted, fidgeting with the IV penetrating his arm.

"Do you want me to finish?" she asked.

"Please," he said, retiring his hands to his waist.

"When you arrived here, most of your vital organs were shutting down," she said. "We had to induce you into a coma. It's truly miraculous that you are alive and are seemingly on the path to being well."

The room went quiet, less the intravenous drip.

"So tomorrow is Christmas?" he asked.

"Yes," she said.

Drip. Drip. Drip.

"But why me? Why... how... why am I alive, then?" he asked, tears now steadily streaming from both eyes. "I'm a nobody. My family is scattered. I am not married. I have no kids. My life has had no meaning, at least not my adult life."

"Mr. Amore," the nurse interrupted. "First of all, that's the wrong approach."

"So... I'm going to live?" he asked, needing reassurance.

"You most certainly are," she said. "The next year or so will require a lot of therapy and the road ahead will have its challenges, but I do expect you to live your life as you did before this incident."

"What about Dr. Peterson?" Amore asked. "Have you heard anything about Dr. Peterson?"

The nurse looked puzzled.

"Well, there is no Dr. Peterson who works here, Mr. Amore, if that's what you're asking," she said.

"Dr. Peterson – the Nobel Peace Prize-winning, longtime professor at the university," Amore said. "Have you heard anything about how he's doing?"

The nurse tilted her head to the side and looked toward the ceiling as if giving the matter a bit more thought.

"I've got to be honest, Thomas. I can't say that I've ever heard of such a man," she said. "You can ask our doctor, though. He'll be in to see you shortly. Maybe he knows of him."

## Twenty-Five:
## A Word From the Doc

Thomas Amore couldn't help but cry. He was alone, heavily medicated, terribly confused, and, as a result, was terrified.

The doctor helped Amore bridge a few of the gaps, but there was quite a void to fill. You see, it had been two months since Amore had slipped into a coma.

"Mr. Amore," said a man, dressed from the neck down in doctor's whites, as he entered Amore's hospital room. "I'm Dr. Anthony Millenni. Let me start by saying we are all very pleased by your progress, and certainly I am here to answer any questions you may have."

"Hi, Doc," said Amore, his voice still quite raspy. "Thank you for saving my life."

"Your will to live certainly helped us," Dr. Millenni said.

"Doctor, have you ever heard of Dr. Preston Peterson?" Amore asked.

The question drew a bit of laughter from Dr. Millenni.

"I can't say I was expecting that to be your first question, Thomas," Dr. Millenni said. "But to answer your question – of course I have."

As best he could, Amore breathed a sigh of relief.

"Thank God," Amore said. "I have this long, winding story in my head – and he is my last memory."

Dr. Millenni smiled and nodded.

"Well," he said. "He's been in to see you quite a few times. In fact, he left you a disposable cell phone with his number programmed into it. I'm sure he'll be in to see you before you are discharged, but he told me to leave it with you in the event that he missed your departure. He seemed hopeful that you'd call him."

## Twenty-Six:
## Honorable Discharge

If this were last year at this time, Thomas Amore surely would have made a different decision.

But it was January 6, 2015, and six days into a new year – one that would prove to be dramatically different from those in the rearview.

Amore was discharged from the hospital. Technically, he had nowhere to be and nobody to see. But this was a new year, and change was on the horizon.

Before he exited the hospital, a staff member handed him a care package complete with a change of clothes, a $500 VISA gift card, and a disposable cell phone. Taped on the back of the cell phone was the cutout of an index card with the words "EMBRACE LUCK."

It was a lot to take in.

Amore wasn't quite sure what to do. And that's not to say that he wasn't going to heed the advice on the back of the phone. He had no idea how to operate the phone... or the gift card.

He walked back into the hospital, flagging down the first person he could find.

"Excuse me," he said, catching the attention of a woman on her way back to the check-in desk.

"Hi!" she said cheerfully. "What's up?"

"I'm terribly sorry to bother you, but I hope you might be able to help me work this phone," he said, phone in hand.

He handed the phone to the woman, whose name tag indicated she was Peg Thompson. She couldn't help but chuckle.

"Oh, this old-school thing?" she said, grasping a device far inferior, technology-wise, than her iPhone. "Hmm. Let's see..."

Amore blushed a bit.

"Sorry," he said. "I've never used a cell phone before."

Without moving her head, the woman shifted her eyes sideways toward Amore.

"Really?" she asked. "That's nuts!"

"Well, I have been homeless, aside from my recent setup in the woods," he said. "That was nice."

Again, she shifted her eyes as in disbelief. But rather than ask any additional questions, she figured out how to operate the phone and gave Amore a quick demonstration.

"Looks like you have one contact: Preston," she said. "To call him, press this button."

"Thanks," Amore said. "Can you leave that cued up so that I can call him now?"

Thompson nodded and handed Amore the phone.

"Take care," she said. "And good luck!"

The phone rang for 32 seconds before going to voicemail.

"Hi. You've reached Dr. Preston Peterson. Please leave a detailed message and I will contact you at my earliest convenience," the recording said.

"Uh... hi... Doc... it's Tom Amore," he said. "I don't know where to start. Thank you... thank you very much."

Before Amore could say anything further, something crazy happened – the other line started buzzing through. Amore – new to the world of cellular phones – frantically examined the phone, glancing at the screen to see "Preston" flashing on the screen.

He didn't know what to do, so he did nothing. He stood there for about three minutes outside the hospital door. Mind you, it was January, but his chilly fingers were the last thing on his mind.

Just as he was about to begin the chore of navigating the phone, it rang once more. Spoiler alert: It was Dr. Peterson.

*Green must mean go*, Amore thought.

"Hello!" he said, rather loudly, still unsure of how things might sound on a cell phone. "Preston? It's me, Tom!"

"Tom," Dr. Peterson said. "So great to hear your voice, Tom. How are you feeling? And more importantly, where are you headed?"

Amore was still in awe that he was in possession of a cell phone – a piece of technology he had seen but never touched.

"I..." he said, still pulling the phone away from his ear while examining the bottom portion, curious as to where the voice was coming from. "I am feeling good – maybe better than I can remember. To answer your question: I guess my plan was to head back towards the woods. I have a solid base camp there."

"Listen," Dr. Peterson said. "I have a really, really modest apartment.

But there is a small second bedroom. Are you still at the hospital? If so, stay put. I can pick you up and you can stay here for a bit. We will figure something out."

Amore looked down at his care package and shook his head a bit.

Then he went back to examining the cell phone.

He thought: *Is this luck? Is this what I embrace?*

"Embrace luck," he said quietly, the cell phone held out in front of him.

"Tom?" Dr. Peterson said from the other end. "Are you there?"

"Yes," Amore said. "Sorry. I am here. I feel... I feel... so... undeserving of all of this. But I suppose it's time I started embracing luck. I am here, Preston. Thank you. Thank you so much."

A tear slid down Amore's cheek. He was stepping into the unknown. But for some reason it felt right. And up until that point, he didn't realize that he was without his most prized possession – his box of letters.

"Wait a second!" he said, rummaging frantically through his care package. "My box! Where is my box?"

He tried his best to remain cool until Dr. Peterson arrived. He reminded himself repeatedly to embrace luck and that everything would be okay.

But naturally, when Dr. Peterson pulled up to the horseshoe entrance of the hospital, he couldn't wait to ask.

Dr. Peterson parked his 2012 Mercedes SUV in front of the hospital and turned on the hazards. Amore watched as he bent over toward the floor of the passenger seat.

When he emerged from the car, he had Amore's box tucked under his arm.

A smile immediately extended across Amore's face.

"You have it!" Amore said, beaming with joy.

Dr. Peterson, sporting jeans and a thermal shirt and flashing a smile from underneath his overgrown beard, approached Amore, extending the box in front of him as he got closer.

"You bet," he said. "I did my best to put it back together. Sorry – it's probably not perfect."

"Are you kidding me?" Amore asked, still smiling. "I can't even begin to describe how lucky I feel, Doc. And you bet your boots I'm embracing it!"

The two drove off, catching up as if they were long-lost pals of 50 years or greater.

For Dr. Peterson, it was the emotional high that he had lacked. He was helping someone in a hands-on setting – and it was the man who, inexplicably, had set him on (by most accounts) a bizarre course to being cast off by his wife and employer. For Amore, it was about finally believing more was possible and taking a giant leap of faith rather than sitting idle.

## Twenty-Seven:
## Where Do We Go From Here?

It was hard to fathom: He walked through the front door – not with his longtime spouse, but instead with a man who most recently lived as a homeless, hopeless veteran.

That was exactly the jolt of reality experienced by Dr. Peterson, who knew he had little time to waste in assembling an action plan for Amore.

"So..." Amore said, setting his precious few belongings on the floor of Dr. Peterson's apartment. "Now what?"

Dr. Peterson looked Amore up and down.

"Well," he said. "I guess I should ask you this: Are you still willing to take on new challenges? If so, I am still pretty confident that I can still help you find work."

Amore nodded.

"I am," he said. "I'm embracing luck. New year – new me."

"Okay then," Dr. Peterson said. "I think I have a game plan. Today we can get you a haircut, a fresh shave, and maybe pick you up a few things."

Again, Amore nodded.

"And then maybe we can take it easy for a bit – get you on somewhat of a routine and make sure you are fully recovered," Dr. Peterson said.

"Thank you, Doc," Amore said. "I just can't thank you enough. It means the world to me to feel like I have a friend again – someone who cares."

Dr. Peterson nodded.

"You're welcome," he said. "You know what could be a good way to unwind a bit? When is the last time you've seen a movie?"

"Heck," Amore said. "I... I honestly have no idea. I've caught bits and pieces of things in group homes and whatnot, but I couldn't tell you the last time I was in a theater. It may be 30 or 40 years."

Dr. Peterson chuckled.

"I figured it had been some time," he said. "Perhaps we should get you cleaned up and we can take it from there. If time allows and you are feeling up to it, we can try to catch a flick. And then, maybe at some point in the near future, you and I can stop by to visit a friend of mine, John Coplan. John is the guy I mentioned some time back. He may still have some work."

"Sounds like a plan," Amore said. "Mind if I hit the shower before we do anything?"

"Of course not," Dr. Peterson said, showing Amore toward the bath-room.

With Amore in the shower, Dr. Peterson took the spare moment as an opportunity to reach out by phone to Coplan. It rang... and rang... and about one second before it seemed like it was headed to voicemail, Coplan answered.

"Preston," he said.

"Hey, John," Dr. Peterson said. "Listen: that guy I came to talk to you about..."

Coplan laughed.

"I ran into your old neighbor, Steve," Coplan said. "He mentioned that you are taking that guy in?"

"Took him in," Dr. Peterson said, talking quietly. "I already did. I'm pleading with you, John. Give this guy a chance. I know you still haven't filled that apartment – you know, the one that you are required to fill by way of contract."

Coplan sighed.

"Okay, detective," he said.

"I don't mean to be a jerk," Dr. Peterson said. "If you don't like the guy, we will walk away and pretend it never happened."

"Okay, okay," Coplan said. "What is his name? I need to at least do a little homework on the guy first."

"It's Thomas Amore," Dr. Peterson said. "He's a veteran and he even played some college football at West Point."

"Wait," Coplan said. "*The* Thomas Amore, who was an All-State recruit and widely considered a future NFL player?"

"Yeah," Dr. Peterson said. "That's him."

The name rang a bell for Coplan, who was a lifelong football fan.

"Bring him by on Saturday," he said. "I have a little paperwork to catch up on in the morning, and I'll be the only one in the office, so it will give us a chance to chat."

# Twenty-Eight:
## Meeting of the Minds

After about a week of adjusting to life with a roommate, Dr. Peterson arranged for Amore to meet Coplan.

Despite Coplan's snarky behavior in his last meeting with Dr. Peterson, he was willing to carve out a bit more time for an old friend.

And the fact was: He still needed a "go-to guy" around the apartment complex – someone to change light bulbs, maintain the landscaping, and handle a few odd jobs. It probably also didn't hurt that Coplan, who received government-backed incentives in the rehabilitation of the building in question, needed to fill one of his units that had been designated as "rent controlled."

The more Coplan thought about it, the more Dr. Peterson's plan – as far-fetched as it initially sounded – made sense, assuming Amore was capable of being just somewhat reliable. As long as he wasn't a drug addict, things might work out, Coplan thought, scratching his chin while he glanced out the window of his office.

Amore and Dr. Peterson, meanwhile, prepared to make the short drive downtown to meet Coplan.

"You nervous?" Dr. Peterson asked. "Probably been a while since you've had a job interview, huh?"

"A bit," Amore said with a laugh. "It's been... wow. I don't know. I think I look the part, anyhow."

They hopped into the truck and Dr. Peterson smiled as he looked Amore over.

Amore, who spent the week adjusting to a somewhat regular sleep schedule and life in an apartment, looked remarkably different from the man who'd first crossed paths with Dr. Peterson.

Gone was Amore's scraggly, horseshoe head of hair. In its place was a neatly trimmed "crew cut" as Amore said when he'd asked the barber to bring him back to his Army days.

Gone was the salt-and-pepper beard which, of course, was dripping with blood during his first encounter with Dr. Peterson.

Gone was the piecemeal outfit, replaced by a pair of brown shoes, khakis, and a collared shirt.

The look – and just as important, the smell – of homelessness were now things of the past.

Coplan wasn't sure what to expect when his pal, Dr. Peterson, and Amore walked through the door. But at first glance, Coplan seemed impressed at Amore's appearance.

"So," he said, his smile growing. "You must be THE Thomas Amore."

Coplan walked toward the pair, first shaking the hand of Amore and then Dr. Peterson.

"You were quite the ball player in your day, huh?" he said to Amore as the three stood in the front lobby of Coplan's office, the headquarters for his real estate development business.

Amore shrugged his shoulders and blushed a bit.

"I played a bit of football," he said.

Coplan nodded.

"Well," he said, pointing toward a long hallway behind the main reception desk. "Come on back this way and let's have some coffee in my office. I'd love to get to know you a bit and tell you a little about the opportunity I might have for you."

Much like Dr. Peterson, Coplan found himself drawn to Amore.

For longer than any of them could have imagined, they talked about life, sports, and Buffalo. It wasn't until about two hours of lively conversation that the most important topic arose: how a man who spent a majority of his life in and out of homeless shelters might be qualified for Coplan's life-changing opportunity.

"So... Tom," Coplan said. "I mean... I know you don't have much experience. That seems like a given. But how are your handyman skills?"

The first uncomfortable silence took over the previously chatter-filled room.

"Well..." Amore said. "You wouldn't believe it if I told you. But I'll tell you anyway."

And so Amore shared his recent survival story – the same one that had landed him in the hospital - but he was able to gloss over that part. He described in great detail the lengths he took to maintain his abode in the nature preserve, including creating the equipment necessary to hunt a day's meal.

But it wasn't just the survival skills that impressed the typically not-so-impressionable Coplan. Amore's time at West Point and his service were items of particular interest to Coplan, who'd also spent about four years in the U.S. Army before going into the business world.

"I've got to be honest with you, Tom," Coplan said. "When Preston told me about you and talked up this wild plan of his... I just wasn't sure what the hell to think. In fact, I basically laughed him out of my office. But I can see what he was talking about."

"I told you!" Dr. Peterson interrupted.

"Okay, Preston," Coplan said. "Settle down. Tom, assuming you are interested... Wait; you *are* interested, right?"

"I'm definitely interested," Amore said with a grin.

"Okay," Coplan continued. "Why don't we take a walk around the grounds? It would help to actually show you the property."

For the two hours that followed, the three men did just that, examining the property in great detail, including the one-bedroom, loft-style apartment that came with the job.

Everything seemed fine until one minor hiccup occurred to Amore as they walked through the snow-covered parking lot.

"Would I be responsible for plowing the lot?" Amore asked. "I hope this doesn't change things, but I don't have a driver's license."

Coplan laughed.

"Tom," he said, still chuckling. "Of course that's fine. I have a plow guy. But you are responsible for the sidewalks all the way around the property. And for that, I have an old riding lawn mower with a little plow on the front. It's pretty neat, really. And it's simple to use... no driver's license required."

Amore breathed a sigh of relief.

"Phew," he said. "Well, I don't see any reason why we can't move forward."

And so Amore, Dr. Peterson and Coplan went back into the office to sort of the details. After nearly 40 years on the streets, Amore prepared to rejoin the workforce with a place to call home.

"This," Amore said, tapping Dr. Peterson on the shoulder as they walked toward Coplan's office. "This is embracing luck."

## Twenty-Nine:
## Nightly News, From Afar

Lila Stevenson was preparing dinner in her Santa Fe, New Mexico home. As she often did while cooking, she listened and occasionally glanced over at the NBC Nightly News which played on a small television in her kitchen.

Methodically, she diced a green pepper for a salad. From front to back, with the tip of the knife resting on a cutting board, she sliced the pepper into small strips and then turned the strips to cut them into smaller cubes.

Chop. Chop. Chop. Chop. Chop.

But then the sound of a name she hadn't heard in decades, other than in her own thoughts, rang from the television.

"Next, we bring you the incredible story of Thomas Amore – a man who went from hopeless and homeless to living in a downtown loft-style apartment in Buffalo, New York," the news anchor said.

Stevenson dropped the knife to its side and slowly turned her head toward the television. The program cut to a commercial before she could see the still shot of Amore that had panned across the screen, so she grabbed her mug of tea and quickly ran to her living room, a few drops of tea hitting the floor along the way, to turn on the larger television.

Before getting divorced in 2007, Stevenson had been married for more than 20 years, during which time she had two children: Michael, now 30, and Ron, now 27.

Though faithful throughout the term of her marriage, which ended amicably, she often wondered about Amore. As she sat there on her over-sized chair waiting for the NBC Nightly News to return from commercials, her heart fluttered and images from the past flooded her mind.

A corny car dealership commercial gave way to the show's return.

"Here we go," Stevenson said nervously, rocking a bit as the program's music aired.

"Preparing for and dealing with the effects of winter can be an excruciating experience for homeowners in Buffalo, New York," said NBC's Lester Holt, walking the streets of downtown Buffalo. "Now imagine battling Mother Nature – who has been known to dump more than 100 inches of snow in a winter – without a home. That's exactly what Thomas Amore faced for nearly three decades."

The camera shifted to Amore. Butterflies swept over Stevenson, as though she were a 17-year-old girl again.

It was him.

The nine-minute segment told the story of Amore's chance encounter with Dr. Peterson, detailing what had ended up being a mutually beneficial relationship.

"Dr. Peterson helped you get back on your feet, but you actually helped him a bit, too, didn't you, Tom?" Holt asked.

A bashful Amore chuckled a bit, flashing his recently repaired smile thanks in equal part to dental insurance and a bit of financial support from his new friends.

"Well… I suppose so," he said as he was interviewed at the kitchen table of his apartment, with Dr. Peterson on his left.

Dr. Peterson quickly interrupted.

"He helped more than you know. When he showed me that box of love letters that he carried all these years, my outlook on life changed for the better," Dr. Peterson said, pointing to the box, which sat on the nearby kitchen countertop.

Stevenson dropped her mug of tea.

"This is a dream," she said. "This is a dream."

## Thirty:
## The Snow Falls Gracefully on Memory Lane

A year had passed, and Amore had become more than a local success story.

In the months that followed the NBC Nightly News segment, Amore became something of an international sensation, garnering media attention from as far away as Australia. His rise from a homeless man to a productive member of society was truly something to behold.

But for Amore, it wasn't all about headlines and television appearances. This was far from a publicity stunt.

Although he made several new acquaintances in his year of employment, the personal connections he made – true friendships – brought his level of joy as close to as high as it had ever been in his lifetime.

Angelo Dominico was among those whom Amore now considered a friend.

It was a Thursday afternoon, and Amore hopped off his snow-plow-bearing lawn tractor to chat with Dominico, a local shop owner.

The front of the apartment building that Amore maintained had three retail outlets: a hair salon, an upholstery shop, and a sushi restaurant. Amore was diligent about keeping the snow clear on the sidewalks throughout the facility, but he paid extra attention to those on which the public would walk.

"I just wanted to say thanks," said Dominico, the owner of the upholstery shop, who'd flagged Amore down. "I know we've talked about it over and over. But I just can't stress this enough: You have been doing a great job keeping these sidewalks clear."

"My pleasure, Ang," Amore said with a smile. "Anything for a paesano."

The two often traded jokes, particularly about their shared Italian ancestry.

"But I do appreciate you saying that," Amore continued. "I'm just doing my job and am enjoying every second of it."

After all those years of uncertainty, things were finally coming into focus in all aspects of Amore's life. He felt a sense of place and was mostly at peace with the past, including his relationship with his parents.

Amore's comeback story had a global reach, and it certainly impacted many outside Western New York. But it truly resonated in Buffalo, a city that came out of a construction hibernation almost simultaneously to Amore getting back on his feet.

Perhaps nobody felt the impact of Amore's rise more than Dr. Peterson, whose wife slowly came back around. It didn't happen overnight, but not long after Amore settled into his new home, the Petersons were back under the same roof – happier than ever.

As Amore stood chatting with Dominico that Thursday afternoon, the Petersons and Coplan watched from inside the sushi restaurant, where they were seated at a four-person table near the window.

"I still cannot believe how this has worked out," Irene said, shaking her head with a smile on her face. "I'm proud of you, Preston."

Preston smiled and placed his hand on his wife's shoulder.

"It's been a long road, that's for sure," he said.

Much like Irene, Coplan chuckled and shook his head.

"I'll hand it to you on this one, Preston," he said.

About a minute later, the fourth person returned to the table.

"He has no idea, right?" she asked, joining the group in its collective observation of Amore.

"No," Preston said softly. "He does not."

After only returning to her seat momentarily, the woman once again took to her feet.

"No better time than the present," she said, before making her way to the door.

Amore and Dominico were in the midst of a laughter-filled conversation.

"Thomas," a voice in the not-so-far distance said.

The wind carried the voice toward Amore, whose eyes watered in equal parts from the weather and the sight of the person approaching him.

"Lila," he said.

Shivers raced up his spine. But it had nothing to do with the sub-30-degree air.

Dominico slowly retreated back into his shop.

Thousands of miles and more than 30 years had previously separated the former lovers, who now stood just a few feet apart.

"I... I," Amore stammered. "I can't believe it's you. I have always... I've never... I've never stopped thinking about you."

Amore's tractor remained a few feet away. He shuffled frantically toward it.

"I have saved these letters," he said, pointing to the box under the seat of his tractor. "Through them, I have always had you."

She ran to him, and the two engaged in a long hug, warm tears of joy sliding down their frigid, rosy cheeks.

At long last, Thomas Amore had his love by his side.

*For the Love of Thomas Amore* is the first book written by Charles H. Roberts III.

Roberts, a veteran communications professional and longtime freelance journalist, was born and raised in Buffalo, N.Y., where he resides with his wife, April, and daughter, Zoey. He earned a bachelor's degree in journalism at the State University of New York College at Buffalo.

Aside from writing, Roberts' hobbies include running, kayaking and pretending to play the guitar.

www.ingramcontent.com/pod-product-compliance
Lightning Source LLC
Chambersburg PA
CBHW051302250626
47155CB00009B/3398